POUNDING BASS
a *Rock Chic* Story

by
Kenna Campbell

Layout and design by No Sweat Graphics &
Formatting
Editor: Susette at My Write Hand VA

Poem written by:
Kalen Dion, Surgery of the Spirit, BLESSINGS FOR
A HEART IN BLOOM, August 13, 2020

.

TABLE OF CONTENTS

ACKNOWLEDGEMENTS

From Jenna: To Marion Morrison (Mom) for always cheering me on and Ebony McMillan (friend and fellow author), who gave me the courage to dive into this part of my bucket list. And to my besties, Kimberly Campbell and Kathy Mullins, who save my life daily with their love.

From Kimberly: To my mom and dad, Sherrye and Rob McLaughlin for always having my back, My Elliott for always believing in me and encouraging me to write, to my children and my Sweetsweet - in hopes that they always chase their own dreams... and most of all, to my best friend and co-author, Jenna, for having the courage to chase her own dreams and convincing me to come along for the ride. I love all of you.

From us both: To our musician friends, who were the entire reason we even met 20 years ago, particularly Johnny Goudie, who named Zander's band; Brad Byram, our favorite bass player (and Bex's namesake); Joseph King; and our friends from Deep Ella and Blue October, whose Houston show at Fitzgerald's in 2002 where we met and was the beginning of the wild ride we call best friendship.

CHAPTER 1
Bex

Hi. I'm Rebecca Bradley of the Meadowgrove Bradleys, better known as Bex, much to the chagrin of my snooty family. They're still rolling that I refused to go to an Ivy League school and instead decided to stay in town for college.

While I was there, one day after class, I met some great girls, and the next thing you know, we formed a band! You can imagine how proud my parents are of their daughter, the bass player. That's even how they introduce me.

"Oh, Pippin, this is our daughter, Rebecca... the bass player. Isn't that droll?"

Of course, this isn't said in a tone that beams with pride, by the way but instead oozes with disappointment.

They wanted me to be a doctor. My grandfather was a doctor, my uncle is a doctor, my aunt is a doctor and my mother is a doctor. My dad, however, works in finance.

They were so elated that I was finishing high school an entire year earlier than the rest of my peers, but that elation quickly subsided once I told them that I would not be going pre-med after all, as they had originally planned for me.

I thought that they couldn't have been more upset, but then I announced that I would be pursuing a degree in music production and engineering, and even worse, that I was going to the local college.

You would have thought I was completely ruining their lives. But, it's my life, not theirs, so even if they aren't proud of me, I am rather proud of myself.

Besides, so far I have killed it in college, where I have fast-tracked my way through my degree, and while I'm still local, I'm doing just fine. I expect to graduate next year if everything goes according to plan. I wasn't put on this earth to live the life they had planned for me.

I am living my life on my terms, living my own dreams. I have goals that I am working hard toward, even if I haven't quite figured out all of those goals just yet. But I'm a work in progress, as my boyfriend, Garrett, reminds me regularly.

Garrett and I have been together since high school. We met the first week in 10th-grade chemistry. Mr. Stall had partnered us up to fill out a chemistry chart just to see where we were in our lessons. We didn't get far because Garrett sat through the entire class making chemistry puns. He made me laugh, and I liked it. We became fast friends.

We weren't in any particular cliques. I've always been pretty shy and a bit of a loner. Garrett wasn't into clubs or academics, and he wasn't an athlete, not that you can tell now. He has developed a love for lifting weights and mixed martial arts fighting and wow! Has he filled out!

And he has gotten quite...well, for lack of a better word, he's gotten kind of cocky. He has also gotten even more attractive than the skinny kid he used to be, which probably contributes to the attitude. But I know he just wants me to be the best me I can be. That and he wants to make sure we stay together. Even when things get strained between us, I know he loves me.

But in school, he was as much a loner as I am, if you can consider two people who spend all their time together loners. In the beginning, we were just friends, but over the years we just kind of fell into a relationship. I don't think he ever even asked me to be his girlfriend. I think he just assumed I was his, which I thought was kind of cute, at least in the beginning.

Garrett was always a take-charge kind of guy and that is fine with me. I hate having to decide where we are going to eat or what movie we are going to see. Tate, my best friend in the entire world, gets aggravated that Garrett never even asks what I want to do, but he knows me. Choices make me anxious and I'm always afraid I'll pick wrong. I'm happy with whatever as long as it involves fries. And I've become quite the Mixed Martial Arts fan, which would not have happened without him.

But my true love is my band, Rock Chic. As I mentioned earlier, music is my dream, my future. It's funny how life works. I kind of knew all of the girls, from either seeing them around school or just around town. Then in just one night, we became a family. I almost feel like it was fate.

The local diner had this early 2000s throwback talent night, each of us signed up with our instruments, and the next thing you know, we all got paired together as a group. Our chemistry was impeccable! We immediately knew that this was what we were supposed to be doing. Then La joined up with us and here we are!

My best friend in the entire world, as I mentioned before, is Tatum Miller, but we just call her Tate. She is the lead singer of our band and my musical soulmate. We play well off of one another, complementing one another's strengths and weaknesses.

I often strive to be like her, asking myself, "*What would Tate do?*" before I make a decision. She's very protective of me but also calls me out on my bullshit. She's like a big sister, except that she doesn't even make me mad.

I never hesitate to go to her for advice and she never hesitates to be one hundred percent honest with me. For instance, she cannot stand my boyfriend. Those two are like oil and water. Hopefully, that will change because I expect to share my life with him. If not, I've wasted the past five years.

CHAPTER 2
Garrett

Babe, I mean Bex, and I met at Briarwood Day School. It's the Holy Grail of pretentious private schools in Meadowgrove, New York. That's not the cool part of New York. It's upstate, where most of the lawns are perfectly kept in a cookie-cutter suburban hellscape. A place where we pretend that nothing ever goes wrong and where all the best dreams go to die.

Anyway, I was just this kind of a geeky kid in school, or maybe I was just socially awkward, who knows? But I first noticed her when we were freshmen. She didn't have a clue who I was, but I knew all about her, or at least, the important stuff, or what is important to me. She was super hot.

I finally lucked out in our sophomore year, though, thanks to Mr. Stall, who made us Chemistry lab partners. It gave me the perfect opportunity to get her to notice me. Luckily, she likes to laugh and I am a pretty funny guy when I want to be, if I do say so myself. Particularly when I'm nervous, I just can't stop cracking jokes.

So, over time, we got close, first as friends and then more. We were both always the misfits, so we are a good match. I've often thought that, if she finally straightens up and acts right, I will probably make her Mrs. Cox. Not right away, of course but before too long.

Definitely, before she gets too caught up in this ridiculous band that she has joined. They've been together for over a year now. I thought it was just a phase and that she would get bored and move on to something new. I even offered to pay for cooking classes if she was looking for something to do with her free time, but she wasn't interested.

She wants to focus on her band, though, and of course, school. I want wife material, she wants to be a rockstar or some shit.

I was, however, able to talk her into going to college here instead of going to one of those big, fancy, out-of-state colleges that her parents wanted her to go to so that we could spend more time together. So, that was cool, I guess. Except that wasn't how it originally worked out for us. She got so caught up in practice, playing gigs, and her best friend, Tate, that we didn't hang out as much as I had thought we would.

I had to force the issue, and now I have more time with her. It's still not as much as I would like, which annoys me. When we're together, I notice the things that she does not necessarily even see. For instance, when we walk down the street, guys would turn to check her out. They couldn't even give me the respect that is due to me as her man. It made me so angry that I wanted to punch something.

That anger was the main reason I started working out. It helped me focus and let it out. I ended up getting pretty buff in the process, which was a very nice bonus. Now, she still gets too many guys trying to look at her but most just sneak a quick peek, because they're too intimidated by my biceps, that I often keep tightly wrapped around her, just in case anyone has a memory lapse and forgets who she belongs to.

Of course, it's hard for me to think about her being in this band. It's five seriously attractive babes dressed up sexy and rockin' out. They're just asking for both attention and trouble. So, I make sure I am there for every single show, no matter how miserable it makes me. Hell, I'm even at every damned, god-forsaken practice.

There are so many things I would rather be doing, but I'm left bored and pissed off, while she's up there looking like a slut. I'm just expected to take it. She has no clue how lucky she is to have me around. No other guy on the planet would put up with half of the garbage that I'm subjected to.

Honestly, I feel like she's letting her friends take away my control and I'm forced to just go along for the ride. I know that I'm nearing my breaking point with this crap, and I'm going to have to make her quit the band before it goes much further. Frankly, she'll need to just quit the music business altogether. Those girls are bad influences on her.

You can't be a good wife and mother in this environment. Obviously, something is going to have to give.

CHAPTER 3
Bex

What a night! The room is electric and we killed our set. The crowd was going wild singing our songs! Our songs! The ones we've spent hours composing and practicing. These songs are our babies and the crowd loves them.

Everyone is happy. Well, almost everyone, Garrett, as usual, is sitting at the bar, staring down into his drink and ignoring everything and everyone around him. I'm not sure exactly when things changed, he's just always either sulking or mad at me about something. I may not know why or how, but he always makes sure that I know everything is my fault.

I spend our time together walking on eggshells around him and I'm always on guard, trying to make sure that I don't do anything to piss him off. The only problem is that I never know what will be setting him off at any given moment. I do know that he hates that I'm in a band, but I had to do something for myself. Music is my dream, it's one of the few things that bring me joy, so damn the consequences.

However, he has vowed to be at every show because... well, groupies. Is there even such a thing as male groupies? I'm not sure that there is when there isn't any money or fame involved, but I am sure about one thing. Garrett is set on sucking the enjoyment out of my shows, and as much fun as I have to play, I keep myself reserved. It takes away from the full experience. Still, I wouldn't trade my time on stage for anything.

I help pack away my equipment and then make my way out to Garrett. I go to hug him, but he just sits on the stool, guarded and tense. It's almost like hugging a stick.

"What's wrong?" I ask.

"I don't like the way the men in here look at you. I trust drunk men about as far as I can throw them," he says to me.

"But don't you trust me?" I ask. He just glares at me, roughly grabs my hand, and starts pulling me toward the door, leaving me feeling like shit.

Knowing that it's my cue to leave, I've already decided to forgo tonight's after-party. Both Garrett and I need to be up early, and I'm just so tired that nothing sounds better than my bed right about now. I smile, letting him know that we're leaving, which I can tell puts him at ease. He was ready to go home, too.

So I begin to say my goodbyes to anyone I could between the bar and the door, thanking the sound and lighting guys, thanking the club manager, and the bartenders, greeting and thanking fans as we make our way out toward the door. Some fans touch my hand or my arm, and I can feel the atmosphere around Garrett thickening.

I know he's annoyed with me, but I do have to network. This is part of the job, after all. As we get closer to the exit, I felt his hand tighten around mine as he jerked me forward to make me go faster. I didn't think too much of it, just figured he was growing a bit impatient to be on our way home. As we approached his car, however, he rounded on me. I could tell from his facial expression that he was angry.

"What's wrong?" I asked.

"You always do this. You flirt with some guy and then act innocent about it. Is that why you didn't want to tell me about the after-party? Were you going to meet up with him?" he spoke through tightly clenched teeth as he spit the words at me, but I just stood there, confused and bewildered.

My silence made him even more upset, but I was trying to piece together my thoughts before I spoke.

"Nothing to say, Bex? Trying to think of a quick lie? I saw the way you two looked at one another! He might as well have ripped your clothes off right then and there!" he yelled, no longer trying to hide his anger.

Stragglers in the parking lot started to turn their heads in our direction. I felt my cheeks heat up at the sudden awkward attention we were receiving. But no one approached. They just watched from a distance. I have never been so embarrassed in my life.

"You can find your own way home," he said, his voice falling flat and nonchalant like he hadn't just been screaming at me in front of 20 other people. "Maybe your new boyfriend will give you a ride."

He started to get into his car without me when I stumbled over in my confusion.

"What are you talking about? What guy? I wasn't going to the after-party. I was going home. You were driving me to my house!"

"Yeah, so he could come to pick you up!" he yelled at me as he slammed his door and drove away, leaving me alone in the parking lot.

I turned to see if anyone else I knew was there, but I didn't recognize any of the people lumbering about. Between the blurriness of my tear-filled eyes, and the parking lot swollen with cars, I just gave up, turned and started walking in the direction of my home. Thankfully, I remembered my key and my house is only a mile and a half away.

As I approached my first turn, the wind began to pick up and I felt a few light sprinkles. I was beginning to regret not bringing a jacket with me tonight. I knew it would be cold, but the stage gets heated and I had planned to go straight home afterwards, so I didn't think it was necessary.

I picked up my pace to get home before the rain grew heavier, but unfortunately, within minutes the rain was beating down hard. I'm so tired that I just find my body slowing down, which is giving me more time to think about my predicament.

I'm cold, tired, drenched to the bone, and I just want to be home already. I don't know how I get myself into these situations, but here we are again. All I wanted was to have a night of music and fun with my best girlfriends, and we certainly had a great time. But somehow, I managed to upset Garrett, again.

As I continue my trek home in the rain, I catch myself replaying the night over and over in my head, trying to filter out the exact moment I did something wrong. Who was this guy he said I flirted with? I try not to even make eye contact with anyone and I always try to keep my conversations with new people very brief.

I continue to think about it and I realize that there was a brief moment, a warm hand squeezed mine in a way that did catch my attention. I looked up and met someone's eyes very quickly and looked away. His eyes were intense though. Is that the moment that set Garrett off? I didn't flirt with anyone, but now that I'm replaying it in my mind, I catch my breath hitching at the memory of how stunning they were and how warm his hand was.

It just didn't register at the time, but maybe Garrett was actually onto something for once. Of course, I would have never thought of him again if Garrett wasn't insisting I was flirting. But now.... now I can't stop thinking about that moment, or more specifically, about a gorgeous set of eyes and a soft, warm hand.

I turn the final corner to my street. Relief fills me and gives me a second wind as I see my parents' enormous house lit up by a couple of large, bright, black lanterns at the front door. As I stumble in through the doorway, I begin to peel my wet clothes off and let them fall onto the floor. Deciding I'll deal with my clothing in the morning, I make my way to my soft, warm bed. I lift the blankets as they invite me inside, enveloping me to drift off into a cozy slumber but not before I begin to hear the vibrations of my phone on my nightstand.

I tightly pull the pillow over my ears to try to drown it out but to no avail. My mind won't rest, and I'm too busy thinking about what his texts say. Knowing that when I look, he'll either act like nothing happened, or he'll accuse me of some new slight. Or both. My curiosity won't let me rest, I feel my heart thumping against my chest, anxiety creeping in as I glance at my phone.

Hey, Hun. Did you make it home safely? It was raining and I was so worried about you.

Interestingly, he's decided to play the 'It never happened' card tonight.

I'm safe. But I'm very tired. Going to sleep. I text back.

Then I quickly add *I love you*, knowing full well that if I don't, it will quickly escalate.

I love you, too. Goodnight, he responds.

With that, my eyes fall heavy and I drift off to a sound sleep.

CHAPTER 4
Zander

Normally I only go to the club for sound check, which just takes a little while, then head back to the hotel and out to eat at the closest fast food place I can find, or I head home for a quick meal if it is a local gig, both options giving me a chance to decompress before the show.

I usually try to avoid opening bands like the plague, but something about this band's look makes me curious. Five hot chicks with instruments. What can be better than that? Hot chicks with both instruments AND talent. I hope they are worth missing dinner for because I am starving.

But one of them has piqued my interest and now I think I need to check them out. She has short dark hair and manages to look innocent while simultaneously looking like she has a hard-ass vibe. I'm not sure which side to believe. I'm not sure which side to buy into, but I think I might want to find out. Something in her eyes makes her look sad, though, and it makes me want to protect her.

I order a drink at the bar and politely say hello to the man sitting to my right. He glares at me and turns away. He reminds me of Michael's brother on the show Prison Break. Man, I loved that show. The character I'm thinking about is a big guy, bald and with solid muscle. I wish I could remember the character's name, but it doesn't really matter. So I smile and nod as thanks to the bartender when he returns,, toss a couple of bucks in the tip jar, grab my drink and make my way toward a table in the back. I am hoping these chicks live up to their band's name:

*****

Holy hell. These girls are good. They will be signed before you know it. Shit, we may open for them someday. I've kept my eye on the bass player in particular. I love the way she pounds that bass. The way she slaps it reminds me of Flea from Red Hot Chili Peppers. She is talented.

They all are and she's also incredibly stunning and I can't keep my eyes off of her. I try not to stare, but it's next to impossible to keep my eyes off someone so beautiful. I have to meet her. The sadness stays in her eyes while she plays, but there is a strength that vibrates through those very aggressive basslines she's putting out.

When their set ends, it's time for me to move toward the stage for our set. I want to go toward her to say hello, maybe get a better reading on her. I hope to finally figure out whether it's the innocence or the hardass that is getting so much of my attention.

However, it looks like she's making a beeline toward the bar and straight for the beefcake guy I noticed earlier. Well, shit. He's grabbing her arm and trying to tug her toward the door.

I only have a chance to shake her hand and tell her it was a great performance, and I'm not even sure she heard me. Oh well. Honestly, It's probably for the best. The last thing in the world that I need right now is a girlfriend, especially a fellow musician. Besides, I have a lot going on outside music anyway, I just don't have the time to worry about girls.

I walk up the small set of stairs to the stage and start scanning the crowd. The bar is a smaller venue, but it feels packed. I'm fairly certain we're breaking a few fire codes at this point.

Walking toward the microphone, I hear the murmurs get louder and louder until they turn into full-blown cheers, screams, and whistles. Every time it's a surreal experience. I don't know if I'll ever get used to the feeling, and I don't know that I would ever really want to. If I'm being honest, being on stage is the best, most pure high you can get.

Our drummer starts in with a low beat, and I slowly slide my hands around the microphone. I feel myself transform into my stage presence, channeling the Rolling Stones.

I ooze into the mic, "I see our usual losers, boozers, and misfits are all here!"

The crowd only gets louder, and I feel their energy flowing through me. I love my real job. It's rewarding, but it's hard and I carry that work home with me every day. On nights that I can step out onto the stage,

I can put it away for a few hours and get lost in the crowds and the music. It's intoxicating.

"So what did you think of our opening band?"

I hear the loud whistles and yells of approval.

"Yeah, me too, man. Me too," I say as the drum intro begins to swell behind me.

The stage lighting quickly changes, and the lights over the crowd begin to fade out as I lean into the mic, and muscle memory takes over.

To the left of me, I see our bassist, Tommy swaying cooly back and forth, he always looks bored, but I know for a fact that he loves every minute of it. Behind me, Harris carries the entire song, keeping us on tempo as he wildly bangs on the drums, and to the right of me, my little brother Ethan is grinning like a fool as he kills it on lead guitar. I sing, I play rhythm guitar, and I write songs. But these guys keep me going. I could not do this without them. I wouldn't do this without them.

Tonight, though, I feel a little off. I feel like I'm losing some focus. My mind keeps thinking about the girl, her meathead boyfriend and the way he was pulling her. There was something about it that wasn't sitting well with me.

After our set, I smiled and nodded to everyone I passed, but my mind was on finding the club owner, Hawthorne. I wanted more information about our opening band.

I reasoned with myself that I wanted to work with them more, but in the back of my mind, I knew that wasn't the only reason I needed to know about them.

Hawthorne was in the backroom, loading up a box of vodka to take the front. I grabbed the box to help him as I started talking him up.

"So, our opening band was cool."

"Oh, Rock Chic? Yeah, those girls are amazing. I'm really impressed with them," he said, before adding, "I'm definitely going to get them back in soon."

"Well, the guys and I would like to do another show with them. Maybe do a little work together, or something."

I was trying to sound interested but not too interested.

But I am pretty certain Hawthorne saw right through me because he chuckled, slapped my shoulder, and said, "Come on, Zan. Let me take you to meet Tate. Pretty sure she's still hanging around out front."

I wasn't sure who Tate was exactly, but I was interested.

As I followed him out, I noticed a few of their band members were still hanging out, and my guys were standing right in the middle of them all. You could tell by Ethan's big smile he was enjoying being surrounded by so many attractive ladies.

But, that was my little brother, always smiling. I envy him. That kid finds joy in everything. Hawthorne walked to the group.

"Tate!" he loudly exclaimed with a big smile on his face. "I see you've already made acquaintances with the rest of the guys. This is Zander."

Hawthorne firmly tapped my shoulder, winked at me, and walked away. I look toward both of the groups already hanging out, relieved that this might be easier than I had thought.

CHAPTER 5
Bex

The morning light begins to creep through my curtains, but I'm so tired I just try to clamp my eyes a bit tighter to stay asleep. My body is still exhausted from my impromptu walk home last night after performing for a little over an hour, and I'm just not quite ready to crawl out of bed.

Suddenly I remember that Tate is picking me up this morning. We're grabbing breakfast at the diner and then heading over to Mulligan's Music Haus, where I like to daydream about the bass guitars hanging on their wall.

There is one in particular that I've had my eye on for months. It's expensive for an old used bass, but it's a classic. 1988 Alembic Stanley Clarke Signature in all its natural flamed walnut glory! It costs as much as a used car, but I've been saving for a while and I'm about halfway there at this point.

However, there is only one, and while there are several beautiful guitars there that I wouldn't be upset about owning, this one is my actual dream guitar and absolutely worth the effort.

I reach over to my nightstand and feel around for my phone, peek at it with one squinty open eye and notice that it is already 8:15 AM, Tate will be here in about 15 minutes and she is nothing if not prompt. I notice a text, pull it up, and it's from her.

It says, *On my way! Be ready!*

With that, I quickly jump out of bed and throw myself in the shower, without giving it time to even warm up. Nothing wakes you up faster than a freezing cold shower in the middle of a New York winter! I just washed my hair, quickly dried off, ran into my bedroom naked, and hurriedly got dressed by grabbing the first things my hands landed on in the closet.

I am all about wearing comfortable clothes when I'm not on the stage, so I know I'll be happy with whatever I grab. I grabbed a dark blue pair of jeans, a red flannel long-sleeved pullover, my purple striped hoodie, some thick mismatched socks, and my dark purple Converse. I didn't even brush my hair.

As I run toward the door, I grab my knit beanie and my cute little black cat backpack and open it just in time to see my best friend raising her hand to knock. She just laughs and rolls her eyes at me, then we both head toward her car.

As she turns on her car, Halestorm is blaring, of course, which is fine with me. But she stops to look at me, her normally calm hazel eyes look like a brewing storm. She leans forward and turns the music down but never takes her eyes off of me. I'm normally not uncomfortable with Tate, but there is an odd static in the air and I feel my stomach begin to churn in response.

I'm taken aback, so I hesitate briefly before asking, "Everything okay?"

She looks away from me for a moment, and I know that she's trying to choose her words deliberately, which causes me to worry even more. As the silence lingers, I'm thinking of every worst-case scenario in my head because normally Tate just says whatever is on her mind. It's a rare moment when she hesitates.

"Well," she starts, looking equally as uncomfortable as I feel before she completely changes back to the normal take-charge girl I know and love. "Listen, Bex, I saw you and Garrett last night. I saw the way he grabbed your arm and pulled you, and frankly, I'm concerned."

At first, I just stare at her for some time trying to take in what she is saying. For some reason, I feel like a child who has just been caught doing something wrong. Logically, I know she's being protective and is upset with Garrett. Despite logic however, I feel ashamed. I just sit there quietly trying to process my feelings and what she is saying to me, as she continues.

"Honestly, it's been going on a while. He's always dictating what you are and are not allowed to do, he complains about you being in the band, about us being friends. He's tried to push you into things that you're not wanting to do, made you go to school where he wanted you to go.

He yells at you, then gaslights you all the time, blames literally everything that goes wrong on you, and now I see him manhandling you?

He was lucky I was so far across the club last night. By the time I was finally able to get across the room, you were both gone already! I tried to call but you didn't answer. I saw Garrett at the after-party and he said..."

I interrupted, "Wait, what? He was supposed to be going straight home."

I felt my cheeks getting heated and my heart rate picked up. I can't believe he would put me through all of that nonsense last night, just to go to the party himself!

"He doesn't trust you, Bex. He flat out said he wanted to make sure you didn't show up. He just sat there sulking the entire night, looking pissed off in the corner while he sipped on his beer."

I was fuming. I wanted to call him right then and there to break up with him, but the thought filled me with fear.

"He made me walk home alone last night, in the cold and rain, all because he thought I flirted with someone. He accused me of making plans to go to the party with some unknown guy, but he went himself?

He texted me later that night just to make sure I was all right and told me he loved me. He acted as if nothing had happened, but he was checking up to make sure that I wasn't at the party? That is..." I paused.

I don't know what exactly it is right now, my mind is racing with anger. So I just shook my head and looked out the window. I felt my eyes growing hot, I felt them filling with tears, and I didn't want anyone

26

to see me like that. I felt weak. I felt helpless and frustrated, I felt stupid and small. A part of me hates him for making me feel this way, and the other part of me feels guilty for feeling this way.

"Bex, this isn't healthy. He isn't healthy for you. And after last night, I'm afraid for you. It was bad enough when he was controlling you and raising his voice. Then he started calling you names and insulting you, and now, Bex, he's grabbing you like that? What's next?

It seems to just be getting more and more aggressive, and frankly, I'm afraid you're going to get hurt." This time it was Tate starting to tear up.

"You're right. I need to think about it though, Tate. We've been together for so long at this point, and I feel...trapped. I need to make plans, I need to think about what I'm going to do and how to do it," I said.

I leaned in and rested my head on her shoulder, and she leaned into me and gave me a small hug.

"I'm starving! I require waffles!" I said. We laughed and drove off toward the diner.

The diner is special to us, it's where we first became a band, after all. Plus, they have the absolute best waffles around. They also have the best french fries, but it's a bit too early for those.

Both of us order the waffles and a pot of coffee to split, but after the conversation in the car, our weekly breakfast is rather silent. I think we're both lost in our thoughts about the situation. I know she's right, but I'm afraid.

I haven't known life without Garrett for five years! The idea of being alone is terrifying. Or what if I end up dating someone worse? What if I stay and he does get worse? I wouldn't want to do this forever with him. I don't look at him and see any real future, or at least not one that I want for myself. But, a future without him is also terrifying. I look over at Tate and try to imagine what she's thinking. I suspect it involves duct tape and a shovel.

We finish breakfast, Tate sneakily pays the check when I run to the ladies' room, of course. And then we head over to the music store. We love this place, it's like a warm hug, a second home.

The owners are so nice. They let us play around with the instruments and hang out as long as we like. If only Mulligan's had layaway, it would be perfect! I walk around to the guitar section and stand in front of what I hope is my future bass.

It's funny, I can see a future with a guitar but not with my boyfriend. I already know that the guitar would certainly make me happy. Garrett, not so much.

With Garrett, I know he wants a stay-at-home wife, who dotes over him, cleans and cooks, and has lots of babies. I know he wouldn't want me talking to my friends anymore.

Maddy, La, Syn, and Tate would all be out of my life if he has any say. I certainly wouldn't be allowed this beautiful bass. He hates the band, and while he enjoys music, he does not enjoy me playing it. I have no idea why it bothers him so much.

When we first got together, he seemed so much more supportive of my interests. Now, it's always just supposed to be about him.

My thoughts are interrupted when I hear Tate's brooding voice rising through one of the microphones. She's not even singing actual words, just singing. I listen to it rise, louder and louder, cutting through my doubts and tearing me away from Garrett's intrusive heaviness.

She smiles wildly at me before directly yelling into the microphone, "I like this one! I'm in the market for a higher quality mic!"

I can't help but smile back, I feel stronger. She makes me stronger. This is what I want. I don't want to be domesticated. I want to be wild and free like Tate. I want to play music with my band. I want to be with my best friends. All of them. For the first time, I feel sure about what I want to do. I still don't know how to get there. I don't know what steps to take. But, I have a direction.

CHAPTER 6
Bex

I leave Mulligan's feeling fresh and new. My outlook feels different, I feel determined about what I want to happen. I still feel scared. I still need to be brave, I'm just not there yet. But, at least I have goals. Tate and I run to the car, jump in, and start singing.

I take over and start singing, "New Rules", by Dua Lipa. It's my favorite song, and it feels appropriate for the moment. My new revelations have given this song new wings for me, a more personal meaning, like I could have written it myself.

My voice is a soft alto, but in the moment, I'm pushing it out of my comfort zone and belting out notes that my voice cannot normally do. Tate's mouth drops open wide, and she's laughing and singing with me, shocked at what felt like a new outlook.

instead of speaking, I tried to shrug Harris off.", this song is me. I think subconsciously I've connected to it all along for this reason, but I just didn't understand why until now.

My phone rings, interrupting the momentum we had and I look down. My mood instantly shifts as I see Garrett's name across my screen.

"Just don't answer," says Tate.

She says this as if it's a viable option. If I don't, he'll come looking for me. If he has to come looking for me, I know he'll be mad. My brand new confidence already feels shaken. I give Tate a weak smile, and she rolls her eyes because she knows me well enough to know that I'm going to answer.

Her reaction makes me feel worse, I know she's not meaning to, but it does. Her opinion is more important to me than she could even begin to know, but I know I have to answer the phone.

She just looks ahead and I meekly answer, "Hey, baby."

"Where are you?" he demands.

"I'm with Tate. It's breakfast and music store day," I say.

I hear the annoyance in his sigh as soon as I mention Tate's name. I don't understand why he dislikes her so much. If he would just take the time to get to know her he would feel different. Not that it would matter. She cannot stand him, and if she got to know him, she would dislike him even more.

He starts talking at me, demanding to know when I'll be home. He tells me that he wants me to cook dinner for him tonight, and talks about a lot of things that I'm not fully paying attention to because I'm distracted. Tate is now having her own phone conversation. She's smiling and seems excited about something. Obviously, her call is going much better than mine.

"Bex!" his voice thunders in my ear making me nearly jump out of my skin.

At my reaction, Tate's head snaps toward me looking concerned. Our eyes meet and it's like we can read one another's thoughts.

"Are you even listening to me? What the hell is wrong with you?" he continued raging in my ear.

I hear Tate tell whoever she is speaking with that she'll call them back; she pulls my phone out of my hand, puts the receiver to her mouth and says, "You're a piece of shit, Garrett," and hangs up the phone.

Our eyes never unlock the entire time. Mine are threatening to spill over. I'm so embarrassed that she heard him yelling at me like that, and I'm so worried about how he'll react to her saying that to him. My phone begins to ring again.

I'm starting to shake at first, but something about her expression makes me spit out an awkward laugh, which makes her laugh. She shuts my phone off completely. I know this won't end well for me. The entire situation is a combination of surreal, tense, and hilarious.

"You're staying with me tonight," she says. "We have somewhere to be."

I know I am just sitting there like a puzzled idiot, but I just slowly nod. She smiles and we finally drive out of the parking lot. I have no idea where we're going, but I'm just glad it isn't home.

We pull into the parking lot of the Skin and Bones club we were at the night before. The dark gray brick exterior with the random neon signs speckle the outside walls in welcome. Tate smiles her encouragement at me, as we shut our doors, and make our way toward the front doors. I notice the familiar car of our manager, as well as La's car and a couple of others in the lot.

It's a bit strange being here in the middle of the day. It's usually much later before we get out here to play. But we're not playing tonight, so I'm confused as to why we're here. Tate grabs my hand and walks me through the door before she lets go to start hugging all these random smiling men.

I am looking at everyone but not really making eye contact, as I'm very much out of the loop as to what is happening, and I'm still rather emotionally spent from confronting so many issues with Garrett today. Our manager, Sherman, gives me a big smile.

"There she is!" he says enthusiastically. He begins to start pointing at each of the guys in the room as he announces their names, "That's Harris their drummer, Tommy is on bass, Ethan on guitar, and this guy here is Zander, he's the voice."

He smiles as he pats Zander on the back. I'm still confused, but then Zander looks directly at me, and I feel my heart completely stop. I know those eyes. I remember those eyes. I very much suspect those eyes got me in trouble with Garrett. I can't actually speak, and I have no idea what I would say anyway, so I just stood there staring back at him.

I barely heard a muffled, "This is Bex!" from my manager as time came to a standstill all around me.

"Uhhhh, Bex?" Tate leaned into me and gave me a light shove, which helped me regain my bearings.

I was suddenly very embarrassed that I mentally checked out like that. But my goodness, he was beautiful.

"What exactly is happening?" I whispered to her.

"Oops! With everything going on, I forgot to mention. They are the group Facial Syndrome. The guys we opened for last night? I know you didn't stay around to listen, but they're really good. The guys are so cool, too. We're going to be working with them a bit, opening up their next few shows around the area, and maybe do a little co-writing," she quickly whispered back.

Relieved to finally have some understanding, I finally was able to act somewhat normal, smile, shake hands and properly meet the guys. I went out of my way not to look directly at Zander. Just thinking about him made me blush and I didn't want to be obvious. Besides, I'm trying to figure out how to get rid of one boyfriend, the last thing I need is another one! He probably has plenty of girls lining up for him anyway.

I look to my left and notice that both of our managers and the club owner are talking excitedly beside the bar. Then I turn to face our groups and they seem to be chatting together like old friends. I feel like I missed out on a lot last night. But then, I usually have to miss out on a lot because I can't stick around after shows. It sucks because it's the biggest chance I have to just hang out with my friends, but Garrett doesn't seem to trust me enough to allow me to do it.

After a while, I start to pick up that they are talking about the party from the night before and most of them, except Tate, hung out all night. I'm inching my way toward the group to try to be a part of the conversation. After all, we'll all be working together for a bit, but I feel like an outsider. I can feel all the glances coming my way, and I know the guys are trying to figure me out.

Finally, Harris asks, "Hey, Bex was it?"

I sort of just nod and smile slightly.

"Why didn't you come to the after-party?" he asked.

I felt my entire face grow warm, I didn't know how to answer that. So I just shifted and tried to think of something to say. I didn't really want to blame Garrett. After all, until I figure out how to get away from him, he will have to keep coming around. I don't want there to be any added friction.

But before I could answer, quiet, sweet Maddy did it for me, "Her boyfriend never lets her go."

I felt so abashed. I know that Maddy would never mean it in a way to demean me or want to make me feel bad in any way, shape, or form. She is always kind. I also know that it's hard for her to speak up in uncomfortable situations, so just saying that in front of a bunch of strangers alone was a lot for her.

Maddy gives me a soft smile, trying to show her support for me. I smile back at her, but my mind is just now trying to prepare for this new hurdle that has been created in dealing with Garrett. He will not be okay with these guys working with us. He will be even less okay if they think, or rather they know, that he is a controlling asshole.

I notice that the guys all seem to have confused faces and furrowed brows, like they are trying to make sense of this new information they have been given about me, when Tate walks toward me, along with Zander.

As he gets closer, I can feel the air grow warm and thick around me. *Get it together, Bex*, I think to myself.

"Walk with us," Tate says. "I hope you don't mind, but I've been filling Zander in on some things about Garrett. Because, I don't think he's going to take you working with them well, and because I'm worried about his reaction. Specifically, I'm worried for you."

Her eyes look like storms when she's upset, so I know she is very concerned. Hell, I am too. There is absolutely no version of this scenario that goes over well for me. Maybe it's for the best, though. Maybe this will force the issue to come to a head and there is no other way out that isn't equally as messy. Still, I feel very apprehensive, I do care for Garrett, even if he doesn't completely deserve it. I don't want to hurt him in any way.

I smile at my friend, "It's okay. Don't worry too much about it, whatever happens is going to happen, right? Besides, this is going to be a great opportunity for us. Zander, you guys are amazing. I didn't catch your show the other night, I had to leave and I haven't been able to make any shows outside our own in quite a while now. But, I did look you guys up and listened to a few songs, and I was really impressed!"

Zander smiled, it was captivating. His smile was so genuine, warm, and big. He made me lightheaded, which is the last thing I needed right now. I had to push those eyes, that smile, and everything else beautiful they are attached to, out of my head.

"Thank you, wow!" he started in response, "You know, that means a lot to me," which we all know is typical musician banter when they're speaking to fans.

I feel a bit silly that I let myself gush a little about how great they were, knowing that I've given that same response in passing to fans.

He then added, "You know, I have to admit that I didn't look up Rock Chic before the show, which, I'm sorry. I just get busy and have a lot of things going on. But, I did catch your set. I normally don't go in early and get to catch the openers, but I was so glad I did because you guys kicked some serious ass!

This is why I wanted the opportunity to work with you. Do a few shows, maybe get some writing and recording done for a song or two. I want to help get your names out there, not that you'll need my help," he winked, which sent my heart into an unwelcome frenzy, "I'd like to be a part of the story when you ladies get big and famous, though."

He flashed that deliciously provocative grin of his. I know I'm done for.

Out of guilt, I turn my phone back on, and immediately it is pinging like crazy. I've missed more texts and calls from Garrett than I thought possible in such a short amount of time. I see that I have some voicemails, but I'm too afraid to listen to them. I do, however, start reading my texts. My mind is racing from the anger I can feel behind them. I feel panic rising in me, and I know that I need to respond.

I probably should not have let Tate hang the phone up on him and turn it off. I was caught up in the moment, in the strength she was sending me by just being there. I could hear her and Zander talking, but their voices sounded muffled and in the background, despite them standing right next to me. I continue to scan through the barrage of indignant messages, letting me know that he didn't deserve how I was treating him, that he deserved better. He was threatening to call my mom.

I sigh, and text the only thing I could think of, *I am so sorry, baby. I had a meeting with the band. I'll call you as soon as I finish, maybe we can grab dinner?*

He responds almost as soon as I send the message off, almost like he was waiting for it. *Yes. Call me the moment you get out and we will meet up.*

A chill goes through me, but I just respond, *Absolutely. I love you.*

"Bex? Bex? Bex!" Tate eventually shouts at me to get my attention, which bolts me from my haze. "Everything okay?" she asks.

Zander has a look of concern on his face, his expression is painted with a combination of worry and anger. It leaves me with the feeling that Tate may have told him more about Garrett than I want people to know.

Part of me doesn't care, part of me wants to run to Zander and let him protect me from Garrett, the other part of me, however, wants to protect Garrett from everyone else, part of me wants everyone to just see the good parts of him, even if I'm having trouble remembering exactly what those parts are. I don't know why. He's awful to me, but I still don't want him to get hurt. But, deep down I suspect that I'm in a situation that no one will be getting out of unscathed.

"I'm fine, guys. Sorry. I just missed a lot of texts, that's all." I try to smile, but instead, my eyes give me away and fill up with tears.

As I look away, Zander steps toward me and puts his hand on my arm, and gives a soft squeeze, clearly unsure of what to do but wanting to show me some sort of support in our newfound partnership.

Tate pulls the phone from my hands and she starts reading the texts he sent. "What the actual hell, Bex? Why would you agree to even talk to him after this?"

Tate was visibly upset, placed her hands on my shoulders and turned me to face her. Her face was softened with concern.

"Promise me," she said, "Promise me that you will not call him, Bex," she gently demanded.

Her request made me uncomfortable. As much as I wanted to say yes to her, I knew I couldn't. If I don't address this with Garrett, I know it will blow up.

"I can't promise you that. But, I can promise you that I'm going to handle it. If I don't, it will just get worse," I responded.

I hated that we were having this conversation in front of Zander, I know he must think that I am probably too much drama at this point, I would be if someone came into our circle and this was the first thing I saw of them!

"Then Tate and I will come with you," Zander stated.

He was so matter-of-fact, not a question, not a request. He just flat-out decided that was going to happen. Normally I would find this very annoying. But in that moment, he reminded me so much of Tate.

I looked at them both, and she nodded and said, "Yea. If you're going to do this, we're going to be there."

It occurred to me at that moment that I wasn't alone, that I didn't need to be afraid. I have my own army. And while there are only two of them, they're pretty badass. I smiled, relief suddenly washing over me. I felt sure and brave. I am determined.

The rest of the time we spent at the bar was significantly more productive, I felt lighter, which allowed me to focus. Tate hums a tune that she was making up, it sounded like a melancholic aching, even without the words to accompany it,

Ethan softly plays a few chords to go along with it and La starts drumming a soft beat, serving as a human metronome, allowing us to follow a steady rhythm. Both Tommy and I play with a few steady basslines and find a couple that work together.

Zander is smiling at us all, before he yells out, "Stop!"

He leans forward toward us and says, "That's the one. The double bassline, do that! That was cool as hell. I think I want us to find a complementary rhythm for the entire thing, two complementary sounds to each instrument, with a duet with Tate and I."

He glances directly at me and gives me a small encouraging smile and adds, "I think I'm already finding the words, too. We can stop here. Try not to forget whatever you guys just did, Tate and I need to start writing."

He turns and walks away toward the back room and everyone begins to pack up, they're chatting excitedly amongst one another and I start to feel like I'm falling behind.

Tate leans in my ear, "Text that asshole, and tell him to meet you at the cafe for dinner. Zander and I will sit in a booth nearby to do some writing, off to the side so he doesn't really notice us, but close enough that you know we're there and we can jump up and beat his ass, if necessary."

She grins at me, liking the idea of beating up my soon-to-be ex-boyfriend entirely too much.

I laugh to myself as I text Garrett, "Band stuff is done, meet me at the cafe in about 15 minutes?"

As I'm walking toward the car with Tate, Zander runs up behind us. He opens the door for me to get in and climbs in the back seat. He's a gentleman, too? The thought moves through me like a current, I have to stop thinking about him like that. But damn, he makes it hard.

We turn on the radio, and someone is just talking. I reach up to change the station but he's reading a poem and says a couple of lines that stops me cold.

> *"Darling, you're not falling apart.*
> *You're getting rid of the pieces*
> *That no longer serve your purpose.*
> *This is a surgery of the spirit,*
> *And it can be painful as hell."*

"What is this?" I ask.

Zander says, "Oh 92.7 is doing a poetry hour right now, trying to expand our cultural horizons here in suburbia, I suppose."

"I kinda like it," I say.

His eyes meet mine in the mirror, and says, "The best poetry has a way of speaking directly to you. That was Surgery of the Spirit by Kalen Dion, he writes a lot of cool shit. You should check him out. I have one of his poetry books if you'd like to borrow it?"

Against my will, I feel my heart flutter. Stupid heart.

I just shake my head yes and say, "Thank you."

I'm still very much feeling that quote as we pull up to the cafe. That flutter is now replaced by anxiety. I'm not looking forward to the next 10 minutes of my life.

CHAPTER 7
Garrett

It's 11 AM, and I drive over to Bex's house. I was going to stop by and surprise her by taking her shopping. My bathroom is looking shabby these days, and I need some new towels. I thought that I might be able to potentially lure out the domestic goddess I know exists in there somewhere, with some brunch and a bathroom makeover.

But as I've been standing here knocking on her door for the past 10 minutes, I'm beginning to suspect my plans are falling through on me. It dawns on me that she is probably with Tate. I think this might be the day that they like to go eat breakfast and stare at music equipment that they can't afford for some dumb reason. I really don't get the appeal.

On the plus side, she should be home soon, right? How long could it possibly take to do that shit, anyway? I decide to go sit in my car where it's warm and call her. It's just too cold to be standing around like an idiot on her porch when she's clearly not home.

I dial her number and she answers, her voice has a lift to it, she's laughing and sounds like she's having a good time. I've been standing in the cold, waiting to treat her to a nice time and I feel immediately irritated.

"Hey, babe!" she says.

"Where are you?" I answer gruffly.

I'm trying extra hard not to give away my annoyance, but I hear Tate in the background and I can't stand her. She just rubs me the wrong way. She's really hot, but she's also really opinionated. She convinces Bex to do a lot of things that I don't approve of and I feel like she's getting in the way of my plans for her.

I had Bex on track before Tate came into the picture. Frankly, that girl is a bad influence. Now, if I wasn't with Bex and was looking for a quick one-night situation, Tate is exactly the kind of girl I would hook up with. She is insanely hot. She's got long brown hair and light-colored eyes. She looks dangerous. Her body is amazing. But, her attractiveness ends there. She's just too bossy for me.

Whereas my girl, Bex, manages to be super hot but docile and meek. Most of the time she falls in line, except of course, when her little bestie is around. Once I finally get Bex in a more domesticated mode, I'll be able to start moving her away from Tate. Things will be much better when that happens.

She starts trying to remind me that it is breakfast and music day just like every week, and I begin asking questions about when she plans to be home, but I can tell she isn't fully listening to me. I can hear the music blaring in the background.

Finally, I shout at her, "Are you even listening to me? What the hell is wrong with you?"

I feel a little bad. I don't like getting angry with her. Well, that isn't entirely true. I mean, I do feel bad, but I also like that it usually makes her more submissive. It stirs something inside of me when she falls in line.

Okay, maybe a part of me gets off on it, a bit. My mouth gets away from me, but before I can fully enjoy the stuttering string of apologies that I'm expecting, Tate is on the phone, disrespecting me and then she hangs up! That bitch! This is exactly why I don't need her around my girlfriend.

If my girl ever speaks to me like that, it might be the last thing she does for a while. Someone needs to shut Tate up, once and for all. What she really needs is a strong man, who won't put up with any of her shit, to finally put her in her place. I would love to see that!

I call Bex back immediately, but it goes straight to voicemail. I am furious now! She really turned the phone off on me? She better call me back before I find her! How can she treat me this way after everything I do for her? After all the hard work I've poured into her to help her become who she needs to be. I feel the strong urge to punch something, so I drive to the gym to try to cool off. But even when I get there, I can't focus.

Usually, I can internalize everything as I take it out on the bag, but right now, I'm letting myself be entirely too vocal as I hit, kick, and punch the sparring bag at the gym. I notice some of the guys working out are stepping away from me a bit, probably for the best, as I keep letting out a steady stream of profanities.

Stopping frequently to try to call or text. I know not focusing on my workout isn't helping me feel better. But I can't help myself. I don't think I've ever felt more disrespected than I do right now. I go in for a few more punches and high kicks, before hitting the showers, my mood as sour as it was before.

Once I clean up, I send one final message, *Your treatment of me has crossed the line. You don't treat the man you love this way. Do better, or I'm letting your mom know what kind of daughter she's raised. I don't think you want that.*

I get in my car and drive off. I'm trying to head toward my apartment, but I find myself scanning parking lots looking for Tate's car instead. Honestly, she better call or text me back before I manage to spot it. Because right now, I'm not sure how I'll respond if I see either of them beforehand. I am so mad that I can feel my blood coursing through me, it leaves me feeling cold. My teeth are gritting so hard.

Finally, I get a text back from Bex. *I am so sorry, baby. I had a meeting with the band. I'll call you as soon as I finish. Maybe we can grab dinner?*

That's right, I think. I feel like I've been vindicated. I'm still angry with her. But, I like it when I know she grovels.

I respond, *Yes. Call me the moment you get out and we will meet up.*"

She needs to know I'm still mad, I want to keep this feeling up, the feeling she gives me when she lets me have control. I think tonight is the night I get Tate pushed out of the picture once and for all. Put an end to this stupid band. Get Bex back in line.

She texts me back again, *Absolutely. I love you.*

I don't respond, but in my head, I'm thinking, *You're damned right you do, and you are about to prove it once and for all.* I smile. Feeling much better. Sometimes you have to go through a little pain to grow, after all.

CHAPTER 8
Zander

The guys and I have been talking to the girls from Rock Chic for a while. I finally get the nerve to ask their lead singer, Tate, about their bassist, and why she isn't around. Though, I already had my suspicion on the subject given the way I saw her leaving the club earlier. I mention that I thought her performance was kinetic.

She laughed and said, "Kinetic, eh?" She gave me a suspicious, yet knowing smile and looked away. "She has a boyfriend, my dear."

Holding up my hands in submission, "Hold on now!" I laughed, "I'm not looking for a girlfriend. I just noticed she wasn't here."

She returned the laugh and said, "Well, that's a good thing, then, because Garrett wouldn't let you within 10 feet of her! He's ridiculous."

"That sounds a bit much," I respond.

"You have no idea," she says. This time her voice sounds significantly more serious.

I find myself thinking about how this newly found, albeit short-planned, partnership is going to survive if a jealous boyfriend is in the picture. I am wanting to work with these women, but I am also not interested in getting caught up in the drama. Just our brief encounter at the bar alone was enough to know that he's a complete prick. I have no idea what someone like her would see in someone like him. Some chicks dig the asshole guys, though.

Hawthorne comes over and says, "You know I love having y'all here, but ya need to get out so I can close up already!"

We all laugh, apologize, and start to leave. One of the girls invites us to the after-party to hang out some more. I don't have to work in the morning, so I'm down. We load up and form a caravan behind Tate's car and follow them to a friend's house. When we arrive, the music is already playing, the air is smokey. Clearly, a few people have had too much to drink. I instinctively go check on a couple of them before walking toward the backyard.

People are partnered up in a random mix of large and small groups, a couple is heavily making out on one of the patio chairs, another group is sitting around another table laughing and playing cards, and then I see Tate sitting with a group next to a large bonfire toward the back of the property. It seems quiet over there and she is the one I've gotten to know the best, so far. So I make my way over to her.

As I approach, she hands me a bottled beer and I sit beside her. She introduced me to a few of the people hanging around, they all had kind things to say to me about the show, everyone was so laid back and cool about everything that, despite barely knowing them, I felt pretty relaxed.

My other bandmates eventually made their way over, said hi, and everyone sort fell into this rhythm of chatter about everything from the stars, to the music, to people that they wished had come. A blonde girl that I had been introduced to earlier but I had already forgotten her name, mentioned Bex and my ears perked up.

She started talking about how it wasn't the same since Garrett stopped letting Bex hang out and how much she had missed her. I looked to Tate to get a reading on the situation, and I guess Tate felt my gaze because she looked right back at me almost immediately.

"What's with that anyway?" I asked.

"I don't know what the deal is," answered the blonde girl, "he just seems like a controlling jerk."

Tate stood up and motioned for me to follow her. I looked over to my brother and signaled that I would be right back, but he just winked at me and smiled. I think he thought something was up between Tate and me.

Don't get me wrong here, Tate is a lovely person. She's pretty, seems smart and level-headed, and she's really cool. I like her as a person. But, I have zero interest in anything more than working with her and maybe becoming friends.

Besides, I seem to have another woman heavy on my mind. A woman that, by all accounts, I know nothing about other than she's insanely attractive, she is exceptionally talented, and she's dating someone that I would like to punch in the face. I have no idea what her personality is like, if she's even an interesting person at all, if she has life goals, or even a fully functioning brain.

For all I know, I'll meet her and her personality might suck. But even if it does, she doesn't deserve to be bullied by some insecure little boy. No one deserves that.

I catch up to Tate and we end up going for a walk around the neighborhood. Well, it's not so much a neighborhood in the typical sense. It's a dark road with houses spaced out quite a bit from one another.

It's quite unlike the typical neighborhoods you find in this area. Tate seems quiet as I walk beside her. I don't know if she's just needing some downtime if she's gathering her thoughts, or what, but I feel a bit impatient and curious so I interrupt whatever is happening to start the conversation myself.

"So, everything okay?"

"I'm just wanting to talk to you about Bex but struggling with what that should consist of. I think it's important that you understand her situation before we all work together," she said.

"Oh, I agree. Absolutely. I was wondering, based on the little bit I've heard, how that was going to go."

She proceeded to tell me all about Bex and Garrett, and how they met. How Garrett controls Bex's narrative, from where she was allowed to go to school to when she can hang out with her friends to the clothes she wears. He decides what she is eating and wearing, pressures her about her friends.

Tate feels like he's trying to get her to leave the band. She says he's insanely jealous. That he sends her angry texts regularly, that he yells at her, and swears at her. She talked about seeing him grab her earlier that night, how upset it made her, and how she tried to get to them before they left but was blocked in by so many people inside the club that it made it hard to get around.

"I saw that, too." I said, "It's upsetting. I've seen it in my line of work, not as much directly because I work in a different department. But, I've seen it through the eyes of my colleagues. People like him only become more and more aggressive before someone gets seriously hurt, or worse."

Tate stands silent and still, I can feel the tension pulsing all around us. I know she's upset.

"I'm so sorry, I don't say that to upset you or worry you more. I just...I don't want to see your friend get hurt."

She shakes her head and says, "No, you don't need to be sorry, he does! You're only telling me what I already know. What kills me is that she is someone completely different when he isn't around. For those brief moments that she's free, she's strong, creative, vibrant, fearless, and amazing. At least, until he starts calling and texting anyway. Just to remind her that she can't be who she wants to be.

You can catch a glimpse of her when she's on stage, the real her, but he stares at her angrily the entire time and she knows it, so the real Bex doesn't fully come out. She's subdued. When he's with her, she's always apologizing. She no longer knows what she wants, she has none of her own opinions, she's timid, frightened and just so resigned. It just makes me so angry when I think of the way he treats her.

He even gets mad at her when he thinks a guy is looking at her. Like it's somehow her fault that she's pretty. Maybe he'd be happier if she just tossed a bag over her head?" she laughed, but it was such a small, muted laugh. One that let me know she's trying to make light of a situation that was heavily weighing her down.

Tate looks so sad for her friend that instinctively I pull her to me to hug her. Worried I might have crossed a line, since we just met and Tate doesn't seem like a particularly cuddly person to me, I start to quickly let go, but she holds on, so I allow myself to hug her more.

My mind wanders to Bex, though. I suddenly feel the need to protect her, to help her. She's so tragic and beautiful, and her friends love her very much. Based on that alone, I knew she had to be a good person. Through their eyes, I am starting to feel like I know her.

"When was the last time you checked in with her?" I ask.

She tells me that she'd been trying to text all evening but hasn't gotten any responses.

"Want to go check on her? I'll drive."

My suggestion seems to bring Tate some relief as she nods yes and smiles. We head back to the house and toward the driveway, but when we get there we run into none other than Garrett.

"I'm surprised to see you here," Tate starts, "Where is my bestie?"

I can tell she's trying to come off friendly, but she has an air of interrogation about her.

"I was just making sure she wasn't here," he says.

"Why would she be here? She went home with you," she asked, obviously confused.

"She didn't go home with me tonight. I drove off without her. I figured she'd be meeting him here," he gestured toward me, but that didn't make sense so I looked behind me thinking he must have meant someone else.

"That is absolutely insane, Garrett. She doesn't even know him!" Then she motioned for me to follow her, and we quickly moved toward my car and got in. "That was weird," I said.

"Very. He doesn't let her out of his sight! We need to go see if she's okay!" Tate said, her voice heavy with worry.

We drove off with her directing me to Bex's home. I was shocked that he would just leave her there, and even more that he thought she would have been with me.

That just doesn't make any sense at all. We've never even met. He must have me confused with someone else. Eventually, she has me turn left on a small, dark road through an upscale but strangely plain neighborhood.

She directs me to pull over in front of a large, white, 2-story house that almost looks identical to every other house on the street. She then goes up to the door but doesn't knock. I notice her leaning in and looking through the windows. She turns toward me, looking relieved, and gives me a small thumbs-up before walking back to the car.

"She made it home," she says as she's getting in the car. She's relieved. "I saw the kitchen light on and her clothes piled through a slit in the window."

"This is her house?" I ask, confused. She just seems more colorful and interesting than some cookie-cutter-styled, yuppie neighborhood.

"Not really," started Tate, "she lives here with her parents."

That makes much more sense, I thought to myself.

"Do you want to head back to the party?" I ask.

"No, I think I just want to go pick up my car and head home. With Garrett around, I wouldn't be able to enjoy myself anyway, and I have an early morning with Bex," she answers. She sounds tired.

"Do you think we can all meet up tomorrow? At the club? I'd like to start working together right away. And it would give me the chance to finally meet her." I smile.

She nods, and then we quietly drive back to the party. Tonight has been all the drama that I didn't want, and yet, I find myself looking forward to tomorrow.

CHAPTER 9
Bex

I walk into the old local diner. I chose this place because it's so comfortable for me. Something about the glittery, red, vinyl booths, the white, speckled, laminate countertops, everything lined in shiny chrome, against worn checkered floors.

The white paper hats, and the waitresses in their pressed, baby blue uniform dresses. Most of the waitresses were older ladies but there were a couple of younger women as well. I loved that some of the older women still kept their big, diner hair, smacked gum and rocked some seriously long nails.

Freshly brewed coffee was consistently making its rounds, I always ordered the coffee, no matter if I was coming for breakfast, lunch, or dinner. The refills are free and they never care about how long you sit there, your mug just keeps getting refilled.

For a long time, it was the only place to go around here. Now it competes with a newer, late-night diner, a Panda Express, and a Starbucks. I think it's going to survive, it's a staple. Though, I do like the idea of the area building up a little bit.

For now, however, at this moment, as I wait for my boyfriend to arrive, this place provides me with both the public spot I need to feel safe and the comfort I need to feel strong, in order to go through with ending this relationship with Garrett.

We've known one another for five years. For most of those years, we were a couple. Even under good circumstances, breakups occurring from a long-term relationship are difficult. I'm not sure exactly what I'm going to say to him.

I have been trying to rehearse it in my head, but instead, my mind keeps wandering to whether I should move and change my number after. While I mentally scold myself for making this more complicated on myself than it needs to be and for my inability to focus, I notice Garrett walking in.

He is moving in long strides toward me. He has a way of making himself look both extremely cool and very frightening all at once. His eyes seem bluer and more intense than usual, his beard is perfectly manicured, and his smile is nonexistent. I can tell by the crease line across his forehead that he is still terribly angry at me, and instinctively I grip the vinyl seats underneath me in an attempt to steady my nerves.

When he finally arrives at my table, for a moment, he's just standing there staring down at me. It feels very intimidating, his massive body casts a large shadow that not only envelopes me but half the table as well. I suddenly feel very thankful that he agreed to dinner somewhere public tonight.

Finally, he slides into the seat across from me and says, "I hope they build a Chili's or some shit around here soon. It'd be nice to eat something with side options beyond greasy fries for once."

Then he pulls the menu to his face like nothing has happened all day. I can feel Tate and Zander's eyes on me, and I just make a strange face and shrug, because I have no idea what is going on right now. He's acting like he has been pissed off with me all day long.

"I know, right?" I nervously laugh.

He peaks at me over the menu, "You couldn't have picked a better spot?"

He sounds annoyed with me. I know we're sitting almost directly in the center of the diner, but that was strategic. However, I'm not about to tell him that.

"Oh, sorry. I just wanted to be sure you could see me when you walked in."

I smile meekly at him. He raises his eyebrow at me and then goes back to the menu.

"Your mom always says you like being the center of attention," he mumbles into the menu.

I tell him that I'm sorry as our waitress approaches our table. It's Melissa, she's been working here for years, and she smiles warmly at us both. He doesn't even look at her.

"I'll have the pot roast dinner with a Sprite... she'll have the same," he says dismissively. I try to interject that I'm not that hungry, I'd rather have the fries, but he just waves me off and tells Melissa that I'm just being silly and I'll have the actual dinner. She winks at him and laughs before walking away.

The people here always think he's just being charming and a good boyfriend who takes care of me.

And you know what? I even like pot roast! I just don't want it right now.

It occurs to me at that moment that not only is he an asshole to me directly, but he controls almost everything I do, and I just let him because I bought into the caring boyfriend routine too, just like Melissa has. I suddenly feel a renewed determination to get through this breakup. I glance one last time at my friends for encouragement and lean forward so that I could make sure he heard me. I spoke to him in a low but firm tone so I could be clear, without causing a scene.

"Garrett, it's over. After what you did last night, and the way you've treated me for years, I'm just done."

He froze, but his expression never changed. His eyes moved slowly up to mine, and completely without any emotion he says, "No."

"No?" I said, as I started feeling a bit exasperated, "What do you mean, no?"

He smirked, "Oh Bex. You're being hysterical. You know that isn't what you really want or what you even need," he said.

He managed to sound both bored and smug at the same time.

"Are you done with this nonsense?" he added, "Or should we ask for the check and just go home where we can have a real discussion."

"Garrett," I said, increasingly annoyed, "You left me to walk home in the rain because you got jealous over absolutely nothing!" I said, trying to keep my voice low but fighting the rising frustration I was feeling.

"You should be thanking me," he smiled, "You know you've put on a few pounds these past few months, right? A little walking never hurt anyone."

At this point I started to get up, I was just going to leave, but he demanded, "Sit down."

Something in his tone scared me and I instinctively followed directions. At this point, I know I need more encouragement, and I want to look over to my friends, but I'm also extremely nervous about accidentally bringing them to his attention.

Garrett leans forward, his voice quiet but tense. "You are so pathetic. You crave attention from men, which is the only reason you're in that ridiculous band with your slutty friends. But you expect me not to worry? You expect me not to care? Without me, you'd be nothing. You wouldn't know what to eat, you wouldn't know what to wear, how to act. You would have been stuck going to medical school to please your parents, instead of doing what you really wanted.

You have no self-discipline whatsoever. I'm the only one who has truly shown they care about you, and there is no one else in the world who would put up with all of your fucking bullshit!" He calmly spits out every venomous word at me, sounding like he was talking about the weather, but the anger behind what he was saying was clear. He looked at me with disgust and said, "I hate it when you make that face."

Just then the waitress walked up with our plates and sat them in front of us and smiled, asked us if we needed anything else and he forced a smile back and told her we were good.

I stood up and loudly said, "We're not good! We're over! Never contact me again!"

Melissa's smile fell off and she stood still, seemingly confused about what to do next.

Garrett grabbed my wrist and through gritted teeth said, "Sweetheart, calm down. We will talk about this when we get home."

He then looked at Melissa, chuckled, and said, "She'll be all right. She's going through some things."

Just then I yelled, "No!" and yanked my wrist away.

It seems that I was going to be the one making a scene, instead. But I didn't know what else to do. I just knew that I did not want to go home with him. Just then he started to grab at my hand to keep me there.

Before I even knew what was happening, Tate and Zander were by my side. Zander stepped forward between Garrett and me. Garrett's false smile fell from his face, as he and Zander made eye contact.

Tate pulled me away, calling for Zander to come as we headed toward the door, and he followed. Thankfully, Garrett just stood there, gaping at us, instead of attacking Zander. I think if we had been somewhere less public, the outcome would have been different.

We got in the car and drove off immediately, and the reality of what just happened set in. And, while I was embarrassed that I was the one who ended up making a scene at the diner, I was relieved that it was over. I sat in the backseat listening to them both reliving what happened, what they thought would have happened, and the various scenarios where they would have gotten to kick Garrett's ass. I laughed, then I cried.

I felt Zander glancing at me with concern through the rearview mirror and Tate crawled into the back with me and just hugged me. She texted my mom and told her I was going to stay with her that evening, as we drove to her house.

I went to her room, crawled into her bed and cried some more. I know my friends were worried about me. I could hear the gentle hums, the highs and lows of their whispering outside the door, but I was crying out of relief. I was safe, and I was finally letting out what I had been holding in for years.

CHAPTER 10
Zander

Tate and I are sitting across the diner from Bex, in a corner booth that is far enough away that Garrett shouldn't notice us but close enough that we can get to them quickly if something happens to go wrong.

We hadn't been there but for maybe a few minutes when he stormed into the diner, scanning the room, obviously looking for Bex. As his eyes set on her, you can tell that he is trying very hard to maintain his composure, but he is quite upset. Bex strategically choosing the center booth was a really smart choice, offering her even more protection.

I'll give her this, the girl is savvy. I've only just met her, and I am trying very hard to convince myself that I'm just trying to protect the interests of our bands' collaboration, but honestly I care. More than I perhaps should. But, it's not just about her, although I recognize that I am interested in her, whether I should be or not.

When I was very young, my mom left my dad. I don't remember much about it, but I do remember screaming, I remember lots of slamming doors and I do remember a couple of bruises.

My mom didn't want us to grow up around that, so she packed us all in a tiny car and just drove across the country. She's worked hard to give us a happy life, She sacrificed so much to keep all of us safe.

I remember at a young age, I promised myself that I was going to grow up to be a man that protected women. That I would do whatever I could to take care of them and not let them suffer.

Then, my grandmother was diagnosed with uterine cancer. We didn't think she was going to make it. But she was so strong. She fought so hard and she beat it, but she went through hell to get to this point, to stay here with us.

And because of that, I expanded my original promise to myself and went into oncology, in hopes of easing that pain and suffering for women like her. I don't want them to have to go through what she went through, what either of them went through.

Both my mother and grandma live with me now, along with my siblings. It's been a great situation for everyone involved. And, given my position, it's allowed me to take care of them the way that I wanted to.

My thoughts are interrupted as I remember why we are here, the last thing I need is to be caught daydreaming when shit is going down. So far, so good, though. Bex quickly glances over and shrugs at us as Garrett studies the menu. She seems as clueless as I am.

At least he didn't come in swinging. I mean, I know he hasn't hit her before, but he has aggressively grabbed her, forced her to walk home in the rain and has verbally berated her. These things tend to get progressively worse, and he is not going to be happy when she breaks things off with him. I must admit that I'm feeling just a bit nauseated at the thought of his reaction. So yeah, I'm nervous and I'm pissed off. No one deserves to be treated this way, and it's obvious by Bex's demeanor that it's been going on for quite a while.

The waitress stops by their table to take their order and I see Bex's body stiffen, which puts me on high alert. I wonder what he has said to provoke that reaction. But the waitress is smiling as she walks away, so I try to relax. Suddenly, she gets a look of pure determination on her face as she leans forward and says something that Garrett clearly doesn't like. And thus the argument begins.

Both of them are speaking very fast. Bex's hands are quickly gesturing around in an exasperated way, and Garrett is very pissed off, but Bex appears to be standing her ground. I feel a bit of pride and start to look over at my table companion to gauge her reaction, when he suddenly grabs her, just like he did last night at the club. I hear Bex yell out, "No!" The waitress is standing there looking completely startled.

Just as I'm about to tell Tate it's time to intervene, she jumps up and says, "Oh, hell no!" and takes off toward their table. I jump up and follow.

The look on Garrett's face when he registers that we are there is priceless, but he doesn't fight it. He lets her go, but his expression says this is probably not the end. If Tate and I have to take turns staying with her when she isn't at her parents' home, then that's what we will do. I step in the center of them as Tate gently pulls her to safety. Garrett and I just stare at one another for a long time. I just want to kick his ass. But, I know that what Bex and Tate need is for me to get them both out of there. Tate calls for me and I follow. I glance back one last time and notice Garrett is still standing there staring at us.

Tate is telling her that we are just going to stay at her place, asking her to call her mom. But my mind is very busy with worry. His eyes watching us pull away confirmed my fear that he wasn't just going to let her go.

I'm pretty sure he knows where Tate lives. It might be okay for tonight. Maybe she won't mind if I stay there, too. Then in the morning, we can reassess the situation. Maybe my place would be better. God knows, even if I'm away, neither of them would ever be alone.

We pulled into Tate's driveway, and I followed them in. Bex went straight to the bedroom and closed the door. As Tate and I discussed what had transpired and she was agreeing to let me stay there, we heard Bex sobbing.

My first worry is that she regretted it, as often happens in these situations. Tate has more faith in her friend than I do but then, she has known her longer. She reassures me that there is no way that Bex will be contacting Garrett tonight and that she would be sleeping in the room with her to help make certain. I'm going to get the couch, which is fine by me. But I suspect I won't be doing any sleeping. My nerves are on edge. Pretty sure I'll just be up all night, watching and waiting.

CHAPTER 11
Zander

It's finally morning. I've been sitting on the couch all night, every time I'd feel myself doze off, I'd jolt awake, walk the house, and look out the windows to make sure everything was in order. Thankfully, I don't have to work today, because I'd be useless. My eyes and head are hurting quite a bit. The lights are off and all is still quiet. I don't exactly know what to do with myself at this point, but I would like whatever I do to involve coffee and some aspirin.

I stand up to go wash my face in the bathroom, and I thought I saw a car drive by slowly in front of the house. Which doesn't sound weird, but I felt my senses go into overdrive. My gut tells me that car had to be Garrett's. My brain tells me that I'm just being paranoid. It's a neighborhood, after all, people drive slow.

Soon after I hear the bedroom door open and turn to see both Tate and Bex emerging. They're both laughing, though Bex's eyes appear swollen still from crying so much last night.

"How did you sleep?" Tate asked me through her smile.

"I don't think I got any," I chuckled.

"Well, good thing we've got coffee!" Tate said as she started toward the kitchen. Bex began to walk toward me. She had a small, sweet smile on her face and I caught myself lingering on her mouth a bit too long. As I turned away, I froze. Bex noticed, and her eyes followed to where mine were focusing. It was that same car from earlier, but now it was at a stop. I quickly looked toward her to see her reaction, and she began to step back very slowly, her eyes open wide, obviously scared.

I didn't need to ask whose car was idling in front, it was painfully obvious. I quickly walked over to her, "He can't hurt you," I said. "I won't let him anywhere near you." Bex looked right in my eyes, and I watched the fear fall away.

She nodded and then softly said, "I know."

I take it upon myself to cook the ladies a breakfast of pancakes, bacon, eggs, and fried potatoes, in part to show off my culinary skills. It also allowed me a better opportunity to watch Garrett out of the kitchen window to make sure he doesn't try anything stupid.

I'm sure, at this point, he knows that he has been spotted. My instincts are telling me that he has parked in front of Tate's place as an intimidation factor. He wants us to know he's there to get a reaction out of Bex.

It's not going to work, though. Tate and I are going to make sure of that. I have promised myself if he is still there when we finish eating, we will call the cops so we can leave safely.

After breakfast, I check again, and thankfully he is gone. I hate resorting to violence or involving the police, but I'm willing to do either or both to keep her safe. We gather our things to go. I ask the girls to bring enough clothes to last for a few days so that we have plenty of time to come up with a properly planned strategy on how to handle Garrett if he will not stand down and accept Bex's right to end their relationship.

I'm also hoping that with Tate and I staying with her around the clock, she will begin to feel safe and hopefully regain some of her self-worth. She has no idea how amazing she truly is. She has so much value to offer, not just to me, or the world but to herself. She's beautiful, smart, musically skilled, interesting, quirky, kind, and she has sound engineering experience. She's a total badass, and that smile...damn. I need to be careful here.

Once we are sure that Garrett has finally given up and will leave her alone, I'll need to regain my focus. I already have so much on my own plate, with work and the band. Besides, I've already had enough of my share of heartache. The last thing I need is to fall for this woman that I've just met. Even if she happens to be everything I'd want in a woman, despite not knowing what exactly that was until I met her. Yeah, this might be a bit difficult for me.

*****

Bex has been sleeping in the guest room at my place for a couple of weeks now. Sometimes, Tate stays with her and sometimes she stays alone. She has been spending time with my family and they all are getting along great, especially Bex and my grandma. Tate has taken on driving her to school and practice, most days. I help, but she hasn't needed me very much for those things.

On those rare occasions she can't though, I drive her instead. I love hearing them play and watching the faraway dreamy look Bex gets when she is on that stage. It's like she turns into a different person, full of confidence and joy. Significantly different from the performance I saw while she was still with Garrett, where he sat silently rebuking her from across the room.

Of course, I hate that her life has been upended by his abuse, but I love the time that Bex and I get to spend together, even if it is happening at warp-speed due to our living situation. Garrett has done a few drive-bys at Tate's house and the club, but either has not figured out yet that she is here or is too intimidated to show his face.

I am lucky enough to have accumulated enough time at the clinic that my schedule is really loose, my caseload is light right now, and most of the work I can do at home, as it involves the more boring paperwork-reviewing cases and keeping up-to-date on my studies, all very exciting things.

I don't even think Bex knows exactly what I do, yet. But right now, it's just about keeping her safe. Our situation is so backward right now, but we will have more time to get to know one another later.

When I'm with her, I try to make sure to show her how a lady is supposed to be treated and respected. I also enjoy trying to spoil her as much as possible. Despite not ever having any time alone with her, between Tate and my family always being around, I'm not complaining about it. I enjoy it.

I just want her to know her worth, and how she should be treated. To help her understand that her desirability goes far beyond her physical attractiveness, or what a man thinks he can get out of her. That she doesn't need to sacrifice her happiness, wants, and needs for a significant other. And that she certainly isn't here to serve a man. I hope to be a part of building her self-esteem so that she can see her true value.

I feel like we're making headway, too. She seems to be coming out of that haze she's been in for so long. But the way she looks at me sometimes, it causes me some concern. I know she's having some feelings toward me, and as much as I love that, I want them to be real.

I fear that she thinks of me as some sort of savior, but I'm not. I know that it might feel like I swooped in and played "hero", but I'm just the catalyst, a protective distraction, while she gathers her bearings, but the strength, the real hero here, has been her all along. Tate and I? We're just the gatekeepers.

She doesn't need a man to take care of her. She's got this on her own. She's becoming more and more self-sufficient as each day passes us by. I love having her here, having her close to me, but she needs me less and less. I just don't know if she realizes it yet. I hope she does soon though, for herself. And when she is ready for a partner again, I hope he's the right one for her, even if it isn't me. As much as it would hurt me, I don't want her to be afraid to tell me that she only sees me as a friend. As long as she dares to be the strong woman that I know she is inside, then I will be happy for her.

Whoever she does end up with though, I hope that they never make her feel broken or less-than again. I hope they do not make her feel like a doll that they can dress up, then get angry at her when someone else notices she's pretty, too. I hope that she never feels like she is owned by another person ever again.

She's her own person, with her own hopes and dreams and she doesn't need to play a role for anyone. I love seeing the way she's blossomed. Whether she is excelling at learning how to run a sound booth, or she's lighting up a stage, she's paving her own way.

The topic hasn't come up yet, but as talented as she and her bandmates are, I know they will be touring soon. As it is now, the clubs they're playing at locally are at capacity, and they have recently started to be offered gigs as the main act, which is so exciting for them!

Thankfully, there is no way that Garrett would be able to take off of work to follow the band across the country and I know that if they were still together, he would start pressuring her to quit.

She would never have to worry about that with someone like me. Truly caring for someone means having trust and the desire to see your partner truly happy. I have no doubts we can be that for each other. I won't pressure her at all. Whatever happens between us, I want to take it slowly and to allow it to build naturally, if at all. But, I'd be lying if my heart wasn't hoping that she feels the same.

CHAPTER 12
Bex

I wake up to Tate's knee abruptly being jammed into my hip. It was a jarring experience, to say the least. I've been woken up in nicer ways. Of course, I've also been woken up in worse ways. She wakes up as soon as she does it and apologizes profusely to me. I call her a bitch, and then we both laugh.

We're still laughing as we come out of her room, and as I scan down the hallway, my eyes land on Zander, who is standing awkwardly in the kitchen. He looks nervous about something at the window, but then he looks my way and smiles sweetly at me.

I'm a bit embarrassed for him to see me like this. I can't imagine what I look like after crying all night, but seeing him standing there, with that smile, softens me. I somehow feel like it might be okay that I look like hell, and I feel....safe.

Tate and I begin to walk toward the kitchen. He is still watching me, smiling, and I can't help but smile back at him. He's just so genuine, it's contagious.

He was so still for a moment just watching us walk to him, that the slightest movement of his eyes and his stillness as he fixated them elsewhere caught my attention. I followed his eyes and saw that he was staring at Garrett, or rather, Garrett's car.

My heart begins to beat ultra-fast, and I'm feeling like I want to run. I don't know if Zander was picking up on the way I was feeling, but right at that moment, he reacted to it. He came close to me and looked into my eyes, and began reassuring me that he would never let Garrett hurt me, that I would be safe.

And as he talked, the fear began to fall by the wayside, I knew he was telling me the truth. I had him, and I had Tate. I've never felt safer in my life and I knew it.

Tate and Zander were whispering a lot to one another as Zander cooked breakfast for us in the kitchen, but I never felt any nervousness the entire time. I knew everything was going to be okay. Over breakfast, which was amazing, they filled me in on their idea to have me stay at Zander's with his family, along with Tate, asking if that would be okay with me.

He says his job isn't super busy right now, so he can do a lot of the work from home. So when Tate can't be with me to get to and from practice and school, he can. Plus, I'd be lying if I didn't like the idea of having more opportunities to be around him. I know I shouldn't be thinking about stuff like that right now, but I can't help myself.

*****

I've been staying with Zander for a couple of weeks now, and I've gotten pretty comfortable around his family, especially his grandma. She and I have developed a pretty close bond, as she's talked to me a lot about her history with her husband. It's helped reassure me that I've done the right thing to let go of Garrett.

I won't lie, sometimes I miss him. But, I've come to realize I miss these tiny moments we had at the beginning of our relationship before we were established. We used to laugh a lot together, and we talked about things that mattered.

But, I now realize that wasn't ever who he was. Once he got comfortable, he started to get more and more controlling. Then, once he was able to exert more and more control, he would get angry with me more frequently and then act like nothing ever happened. Listening to Zander's grandma tell me her stories has helped me realize that that kind of relationship just gets worse and worse.

But, these realizations have also made me scared. I look at Zander, and I have all of these feelings boiling deep inside me, growing more and more every day. He makes me feel safe. He makes me feel cared about. He makes me feel like what I want out of life is important, and that he wants to help me reach those goals.

I can make decisions and they're supported, even when it's something as small as just wanting french fries for dinner, or pizza without mushrooms.

And, that is all so wonderful, but it scares me. It scares me because I'm afraid that Zander might not be who he shows me he is. I want to trust him so much, and I feel like I can. But, I don't even know for sure if I can trust myself. Before I can even think of moving forward in this relationship, or any relationship, I have to know that I can trust myself to recognize when I'm no longer in a healthy situation. I want to trust myself to get out all on my own, without feeling I need everyone else to save me.

But, right now, I do need that. Mom has told me that Garrett has been parking outside their house frequently, watching for me. Dad has talked to his friend, Dave, who is a police officer in our area, and they have begun picking up their patrols for my parents' neighborhood.

Once my parents realized what kind of guy Garrett was, they actually expressed relief that I was going to be staying with friends for a while.

It's funny, I know I let them down in a lot of ways. But, it's nice to know that they support me in this. It's quite touching actually, my parents aren't the warmest people. They don't tell me they love me very often. They are usually more critical, but I know they care about me and just want the best for me. Still, knowing that they are being protective of me right now? It's nice. I feel stronger knowing that they support me.

It's been a major growing experience in my life. I keep thinking about that poem, *Surgery of the Spirit* by Kalen Dion, that I heard when I was with Tate and Zander that first day, and it sits with me. I think of the line often,

"Darling, you're not falling apart.
You're getting rid of the pieces
That no longer serve your purpose.
This is a surgery of the spirit,
And it can be painful as hell."

The message was delivered by a man on the radio during one of the most pivotal, important chapters of my life. I'm learning, I'm growing. I've become stronger. I'm rising. I'm determined. I feel like a phoenix.

I begin to think about wanting to symbolize my own growth, I look over at my best friend, Tate, who I don't know if I could have grown this much without. She's such a big influence in my life, and I don't think she has any idea how much I look up to her. She loves tattoos. She has so many, just all over her. Each one has a special story. She has told me all about them, and it makes each one even more beautiful.

Maybe I should get a tattoo. Something beautiful and permanent, to symbolize my own growth- a phoenix. I start to go and discuss it with Tate to see what she thinks but then stop myself. This is something I need to do alone.

I've been saving money for that beautiful guitar from Mulligan's for a while now, and I'm finally getting close to having enough. Maybe I can save a bit longer and get the tat first. I feel like, symbolically speaking, it would be a massive stepping stone toward moving forward in my life.

I feel brand new. I've come to my first major decision on my own in years. While it means putting off my dream bass for a little longer, it's worth it. I just hope that no one comes in and scoops it up from Mulligan's Music Haus. I'm going to get a big, beautiful phoenix tattoo on my thigh, and I think I want to keep it a secret for a little bit.

Oh! Maybe I'll show it off for the first time at our next big show that we're all doing together. The idea of walking out and surprising everyone there, being bold with the people who have helped me grow both personally and musically, makes me giddy!

We've all been practicing together and working hard on music for a couple of weeks and it's coming together beautifully. It just seems like the perfect moment.

Tate is dropping me off at the school today, but instead of school, I'll just walk from the campus to the nearby tattoo shop and visit Clair, she always does Tate's tattoos and her work is simply exquisite. Plus, she's a cool person, and I don't think I'd trust anyone else with something so big.

I pull up some samples on my phone to show her and save the ones I like best, before going to my account and moving some cash from my savings so I can make sure I have the cost covered.

I feel a drop in my gut, in part because it's so much money, but I'm also nervous. Doesn't matter, though. The excitement and determination I have coursing through me are more than enough to get me through this.

I choose a long, soft, layered, black skirt that flows loosely around my legs, and a fitted black, long-sleeved top with black lace-up boots. Normally I'd wear jeans but I know I shouldn't wear them with a brand new tattoo. I go to the kitchen to grab my morning coffee while I wait for Tate to get to Zander's so I can go to "school".

I feel Zander come into the kitchen and hear him pour his own cup. "Morning," he kind of grumbles out, then slides in the seat across from me and smiles. I can't help but smile back, as I see Tate's car pull up from the corner of my eyes.

I notice his sweater is on the counter. I can't help myself, so I pick it up and toss it on. "It's cold, I'm stealing your sweater," I say as I walk out the door. I hear him laugh. It's going to be a great day.

Tate and I talk back and forth about nothing important all the way to school. She stops and waves me goodbye and I pop out of her car, walking toward the school. As she pulls away, I turn off to the left and head toward the tattoo parlor.

I've already double-checked that Clair works on Thursdays and thankfully, she does. They open shortly so I'll be her first appointment. She recognizes me immediately and seems very excited that I'm finally getting some work done.

Every time I come in with Tate she always asks if I'm sure I don't want anything, but I knew when the time came, I wanted it to be something meaningful. Though, when I told her what I was planning, her eyes widened, and she laughed and asked me if I was sure. I definitely was.

I showed her what I was thinking and she said she had the perfect art for what I was wanting. It was something she had worked on herself but just never got around to getting to do it on anyone.

She showed it to me, we made a few minor tweaks, and then she began to prep my thigh. As she worked, I talked to her about everything that has happened in the past few weeks. I told her about Garrett, about Tate and Zander and how much the band, both of our bands, have really been there for me.

Rock Chic has even postponed a few shows so that I didn't have to worry about running into Garrett, and we've just been focusing on our big upcoming show with Facial Syndrome and writing some music together.

She listened thoughtfully, offering the occasional words of encouragement. Talking about everything made me consider how many people I have in my corner. All of the girls have rallied behind me and shown that they have my back, the guys, too.

"It sounds like you've chosen well," Clair says with a smile, just before the buzz of the needle begins the outline. It's quite relaxing, so I just lay still, lost in my thoughts for the rest of the day.

CHAPTER 13
Zander

Bex has invited me to dinner at her parents' home. I am unsure about how much they know about me, but I want my smartest, most well-put-together foot forward. Therefore, I have decided on the white button-down shirt with navy pants and a tie.

I have these really cool navy-blue cufflinks that my grandfather gave me before he passed. They are round and have these great little brown and silver bicycles on them. Very unique, very Abuelo. He always wore stuff like that.

I wear them only on very special occasions. Particularly when I want a little luck and my grandpa on my side. But, I forgo the jacket because I don't want to seem like I'm trying too hard. And maybe the sleek black shoes? No, the more casual brown loafers. Again, not wanting to come off like I'm trying too hard. Parents hate that, I think. Right?

I look in the mirror, and I think I made the right call, but I am absolutely second-guessing myself the entire time. I'm not great at this. Thank goodness for lab coats at work! I never have to second-guess myself at work...usually.

Next up, my hair. Oh man, my hair! It's always been complicated. It's mostly straight, but it's got a few- I guess I would call them cowlicks- that remain an issue even now that my hair has grown out longer. I wet my comb the way Ethan showed me, holding my hair as smooth as I can, then put the hair tie on tight, just the way my bro told me to do. His hair always looks fantastic. He swears he has the same issues as I do with mine, but I don't know if I fully believe that.

I feel ready, so I head downstairs where my family is waiting. You would think I was heading to prom by the way they oohed and aahed all over the place. "It's just dinner with a friend," I said pretty loudly, so even my grandma can hear from the living room. I love having her here, but she is so nosy!

They were still smiling and making a fuss. My mom was messing with my tie, then she wanted to take pictures of me. You would have thought that I usually looked like a troll by the way they were making such a fuss. I appreciate them, though. I'm blessed to have such a tight-knit family, not all my friends are as lucky.

I begin the drive to Bex's parents' house, and I'm finding that I am feeling more and more nervous the closer I get. By the time her house comes into sight, my anxiety is through the roof!

She has made it rather clear that her parents are quite wealthy and a little closed-minded. They already know that I'm in a band, so that's already one strike against me. I don't know many parents who are thrilled when they learn their daughter is hanging around guys in rock bands.

I know that they will be judging me by my visible tattoos and hair before they even hear me speak. The older crowd always assumes I'm some kind of a thug, that I do drugs, or just plow my way through groupies, but I'm the farthest away from any of those things. I just happen to like tattoos, and I usually like my hair.

When I approach the door, I nearly lose my nerve. The idea of knocking or ringing the bell is nearly too much for me, but I have managed to come this far now. I can't back out if I want this to develop into a serious relationship, and I absolutely do. No one makes me feel the way Bex makes me feel. I'm not willing to let fear get in the way of that.

So, I ring the doorbell and try my best to stop shaking. When she opens the door, I finally let out the breath I didn't know I had been holding in for a while and just smile. She pulls me to her and hugs me tight, then softly whispers, "Are you ready?" I just nod and smile.

Seeing her calmed my nerves, and I felt sure of myself. I don't know how she manages to do that for me, every single time, but she does. Somehow she makes it feel easy.

She leads me through a grand entrance hall, lined with floral art, gold mirrors, pale blue damask wallpaper, and a rather large crystal chandelier, to a massive living room with one of the biggest, most ornate fireplaces I'd have ever seen. The sizable, roaring fire makes the room feel warm and cozy, despite its size.

I know I had previously thought the house seemed ordinary, I think I used the phrase,"cookie-cutter" but clearly inside it was anything but.

"Mom, Dad, this is Zander," Bex sweetly introduces me, her smile made my heart beat a little faster.

I couldn't help but smile back, trying not to seem too giddy in front of her parents but also knowing I was already failing.

Both of her parents stand up. I had brought flowers for Bex's mother. She told me earlier that her mom likes simple white roses, and she thanked me for them as I hand them to her, but I notice that her smile does not make it up to her eyes.

As I turn to shake hands with her father, I notice that he is solely focused on the tattoos across my hands. He gives me a firm handshake, but he doesn't even look me in the face. I know I'm being judged, but I am trying very hard to not let their clear disapproval get the best of me. There is time to win them over yet!

Mrs. Bradley is still standing awkwardly in the living room, before turning away and saying that she is going to take the flowers and put them in a nice vase with some water, and then she needs to check with Claudia, their "house manager", to see when dinner will be ready.

I'm trying my hardest to make small talk with Mr. Bradley in hopes of finding something that sparks his interest, but he is still distracted by my appearance.

No, not my entire appearance, Now I think it's my hair. At this point, any thought that they would give me a break because their daughter likes me has flown out the window.

"Dinner is ready!" Mrs. Bradley announces happily.

I think she believes that if we are eating, there won't be a need for small talk, but Mr. Bradley does not look like he's going to let me off so easily.

"It smells amazing, Mrs. Bradley," I say, as I feel his eyes steady on me.

She simply smiles and tells me that Claudia has always been a fantastic cook. I look at Claudia, smile, and give her a grateful nod. She nods back, smiles, and dips out of the room.

"So, Alexander," Mr. Bradley is starting the expected grilling, "Rebecca tells me you met through her band. Is that correct?" He's watching me carefully now. Clearly, he has moved on from just my outward appearance and is now looking for other reasons to be disappointed.

"Yes, sir," I answer, "But my given name is just Zander. No Alex at the beginning." I smile, trying to hide the annoyance I felt by his need to make my name sound more formal than it is. I needed to remind myself to come off as respectfully as possible but not let him shake me.

"Okay, Zander," Mr. Bradley says sarcastically. "And what do you do for a real job? Hmmm?"

Now I know that I've got him. I've been planning this moment. I knew I could wipe the smug look off his face and the dripping sarcastic judgment from his tongue, so I just smile politely and say, "Oh, I'm a doctor- an oncologist, to be more specific, at Upper New York State Cancer Center."

I thought he was going to choke. For a brief moment, I felt a bit smug, but unfortunately, Bex has the same reaction. I'm a bit surprised at her response, but then I start to think back through our conversations. Did I ever tell her about my job? Oh no, I don't think so. We've just had so many other things to discuss as we get to know one another than how we spend our daytime hours.

However, now that I think about it, that's pretty lame. It's not something I hide, and it's certainly something I feel proud of doing. With everything else that has been going on, it just never came up. But, honestly, I know we should have had this conversation on day one. It's important to me for her to know me, all of me. My smugness slips away, a bit. I like her dad's reaction, but I'm a bit more worried about hers.

"A doctor?" he asks, as if he might have misheard me. I smile and nod, and reach for Bex's hand under the table to reassure her that we will talk about this later. "And you still, somehow, have time for this....band? How is that possible? I know the hours Bex puts into hers, and a doctor just doesn't make sense."

"Well, sir, it helps that I work at a clinic that has very specific set hours for our patients. I do, occasionally, have a patient or two that may run past

5:00 p.m., but it's pretty rare. And I schedule all of my surgeries two days a week during business hours, only on Tuesdays and Wednesdays. It's pretty rare for me to have an emergency, but when I do, my band is set to the side during that time. They all have their own day jobs, as well, so they know and understand the drill. So yeah, I've normally got plenty of time."

"That's all well and good," he says, still looking for something to judge me on. "But, after all of that, do you have any time left for our Rebecca?" he asks.

"Absolutely," I smile and look shyly at Bex. "For her, I make time."

I have no idea why I'm feeling like such a kid, right now. I've made no secrets about how attracted I am to her. But, she is looking back at me, as she slides her hand into mine. I feel like I've just been given a present like it's my birthday. Her hand is warm, but it's her eyes that I feel burning into mine.

I'm pretty sure she's forgiven me for my accidental slight, but I know we still need to talk about it. Nevertheless, I know she felt the truth is what I said about her. That I will always make time for her. At this point, I no longer care if I won her mom and dad's approval, though I expect I might have scored a few brownie points, at least.

The only approval I need is hers.

CHAPTER 14
Bex

Well, Dad obviously hates Zander, which is to be expected, so I'm not surprised that he is grilling him so hard. I did warn him prior that they were basically snobs. But, Zander is handling it so smoothly, though, not that I'm surprised. He has such charisma and confidence without being a jerk. He's downright charming. I don't think anyone who truly meets him has the ability to dislike him. He's just that guy.

I try to make sure to give him as many encouraging smiles as possible. No matter what my parents end up thinking about him, I like him. I like him quite a lot. The fact that he is willing to put up with this nonsense just to be around me touches my heart.

There is no way Garrett would do this for me. In all that time we were together, he rarely bothered to come to dinner and only saw my dad in passing. He has had a good relationship with my mother, but I'm pretty sure it's just because of his family's wealth.

But when Dad asks about Zander's "real job" and he said he's an oncologist and that he is a surgeon to boot, I nearly choked. How could he have not mentioned this to me? That is such a big deal!

It's obviously a very important part of his life, and frankly, I feel a little let down, hurt even, that he couldn't be bothered to tell me about it? We need to talk once we have some alone time. I hope he has a good explanation for leaving me in the dark.

To be honest, I never bothered to ask him what he did. I guess I just assumed the band was his job, a bit like me. But still, this just seems like something that would have deserved, at least, a casual mention.

I do find it pretty funny how Mom and Dad are both changing their tunes now. The attitudes seem to be falling by the wayside. Mom's real smile is bright and cheerful, the fake one is long gone. I haven't seen the real one in a long time, but I'd recognize it anywhere. Honestly, her smile is radiant and one of my favorite things about her. Dad is appraising Zander and now looking at him with at least a little bit of respect.

While I'm a little annoyed he didn't mention his job prior, there is something quite satisfying about this moment. But then, as dad is questioning him about his time for everything, Zander says something that makes my heart stop. "For her, I make time." Oh my God.

Now I'm smiling like a complete fool, but I just can't help myself. I can't stop looking at him. No one I've ever dated has made me feel like a priority before. He's not even my actual boyfriend but damn, my heart will not stand still.

The rest of dinner goes off without a hitch. Claudia is an amazing cook, and while I have no desire to be domesticated, I do enjoy sneaking into the kitchen to learn a little here and there from her, and watch her work. She makes the most amazing homemade pasta noodles, which is what she made for us tonight. This one had prosciutto and asparagus with a lemon and garlic cream sauce. It was amazing.

Once dinner was over, we retired to the living room for coffee. Afterward, Zander thanks my parents for a delightful evening, makes his apologies for cutting out a little early, and prepares to leave. I throw a wrap around my shoulders, proceed to walk with him to the door, and follow him outside. I didn't want to wait until the next day for answers, or else I knew I'd never fall asleep that night.

"Why didn't you tell me about your job?" I ask, while trying to disguise the slight tinge of hurt I felt that he omitted something so important to me.

"Honestly, I just never thought about it. I know that sounds silly, but when I'm with you, you are all I am focused on. I've wanted nothing more than to make you feel special, important, and talented because you are. You're all those things and more. You are a great friend and worthy of so much love. But yes, I am a doctor.

You deserve all the honesty in the world, I want and need you to trust me. I never intended to not tell you, it just didn't naturally come up. But, I am happy to answer any questions you may have...about my job or anything else. My life is an open book, Bex. I would never purposefully hide anything from you or try to do anything to make you feel like you don't matter."

"I appreciate that, but you realize we are going to need to discuss this further. Right?"

He smiles at me and takes my hand in his.

"Absolutely. You've already been through so much. The last thing I want is to make you feel like you can't trust me. You mean more to me than you could ever possibly know."

My heart melts, I can't be mad at him, I can't even feel hurt anymore. I just feel legitimately happy. I feel safe. I feel free. Zander has done so much for me in the short time we've known one another, starting before he really even knew anything about me. He and Tate are my best friends. And despite myself, I think Zander and I might be even more, even if we're not ready to admit it yet.

CHAPTER 15
Bex

One advantage to staying at Zander's house is there are plenty of opportunities to talk. One evening after he returns from work, I tell him I have questions about his job and plans for the future.

"Becoming an oncologist took a lot of time and money. How does music fit into your future?"

"I love music. It is my stress relief," Zander confessed. "I imagine music will always be part of my life, but if you are asking if the band takes precedence over my career, the answer is no. The guys know where I stand, and they all have day jobs, too.

We aren't trying to become rock stars. Everyone understands that we are playing locally and around the region, but my job is too important to abandon. As long as I have guys to back me, I will play though, even when I'm old and gray."

"What made you want to be an oncologist? That's an emotionally heavy line of work. Don't get me wrong, I think it's admirable, and it fits with what I have observed about you. You are empathetic, kind, and seem to care about everyone you come in contact with. I imagine you have great bedside manner."

"I try," Zander says, grinning. "I decided to become a doctor when my Abuela got cancer. It was advanced and although the doctors were optimistic, her prognosis was grim. Thankfully, she came through it and has been cancer-free for several years. I want to be able to do for others what her doctors did for her."

"That is admirable of you, Zander. Thank you for answering my questions," I say and kiss him on the cheek.

CHAPTER 16
Garrett

I've been going for a lot of drives lately, trying to get my head together. MMA isn't working to calm the anger bubbling inside of me lately. I just can't stop thinking about how everything has played out for me the past couple of weeks. My life seems to be spiraling out of control. At first, Bex was just not returning my texts or calls, but now she's straight up blocked me!

For a while, I was able to keep tabs on her, but between the canceled shows and her never being at either Tate's or her place, it's making it hard to keep track of her. I suspect I know who she's with, but unfortunately, despite asking around, I can't find out where the new guy lives. Thinking about them together makes my blood boil! She's my girl. No shitty other guy should be laying his hands on her! These thoughts are preventing me from working or getting anything done. So, I drive. I'm thinking, I'm trying to refocus, but ultimately, I'm searching, and I won't stop until I find her and make her come back to me.

I find myself turning through the familiar streets of Bex's family home. I've come through here so many times. Her mom loves me. I wonder what she must think of what their daughter is doing now. I wonder if they know what a slut she's being right now. I wonder what they would say if they knew she's been with that greasy, dumb, wannabe rockstar. He can't offer her anything, but I can. I can take care of her, give her everything she wants and needs. Him? He'll probably just cheat on her with one of those nasty groupies and give her VD!

I find myself turning down Bex's street and driving past her house. I notice a black sedan in the driveway and my blood runs cold. Something in my guts tells me that she's there right now, with him. I fight the urge to turn around, I have to play this smart. I don't need them knowing I'm here, but I also want to know exactly what's going on inside, if she's even there.

I pull into a small park at the end of the street and park toward the back of the small lot, before walking down the sidewalk to her house. It's beginning to get dark outside, so hopefully that will work in my favor. As I approach her house, I feel my adrenaline rushing through me. My body is ready to kick this guy's ass, my heart is pumping, and my mind is racing. I try to be as quiet as I can as I slowly creep up to the living room window and try to peek in from the side.

Everyone is gathered in the living room, and it looks as if they're drinking coffee. He is sitting right beside my girl on the couch. She is looking over at him and smiling a lot, and it makes my heart hurt. I don't know how she can do this to me. It's not been that long, but here she is cozying up to this new guy.

Given that they're having coffee, he must have been here for a while. I move off to the other side to see if I can get a better angle. Her mom is smiling. What the hell? She actually looks happy that Bex is here with this piece of shit? She looks like she approves of him? Her parents are not the type of people who approve of low lifes like him! This doesn't make sense. I wish I could see her dad's face, that would tell me the most. He hates virtually everyone. Hell, his own daughter isn't good enough, this guy certainly shouldn't be. I quickly move up onto the porch to get a better look.

Crack. The floor creaks with every step I take.

"Shit!" I say a bit too loudly, my eyes dart up and meet Bex's.

She looks panicked and starts running toward the door. Toward me! This isn't exactly how I was planning this to go. I no longer know what I'm doing, as she flings open the door and yells my name at me.

"Garrett! "she screams in a combination of fear and confusion.

Part of me wants to run to her and hold her in my arms and not let her go, just take her. Yes! I can just take her. I'll bring her with me and I can talk to her, make her see my side. She'll be with me again if I can just talk to her about how I feel. I know it. Her heart is too good, she still loves me. I can learn to let go of the anger, even though she betrayed me. The thought is too much for me, and before I can even think, I'm running toward her.

Her parents are rushing out right behind her. Funny, the coward isn't out yet, though. Her parents are yelling something at me, but I can't even understand them. All the blood is rushing too quickly through my brain and ears. I can barely think straight. Before I know what I'm doing I reach out and grab Bex's wrist and pull her toward me but she's resisting me. I'm dragging her toward the road. This isn't the plan. It's not happening the way I need it to.

"Bex! I'm sorry! I'm sorry! I just need you to lis..." but before I can get the words out, something hard makes contact with my right jaw. Instinctively, I let Bex go and turn toward whatever hit me, but it was him. The bastard who thinks he can steal my girl! I turn toward him ready to fight. I train for this shit. I love this shit!

In the background, I can hear people shouting, but I'm not listening to what they're saying. I'm solely focused on my opponent. His mouth angrily tightens, his brows furrow, he looks like he wants to kill me. I, however, cannot stop smiling. I've wanted this for a long time, after all. I clench my fists and tuck my thumb in tightly. I don't know if he knows that I've trained for this, but he's about to find out.

I feel like toying with him a bit first, so I only land a few jabs across his face and chest. He keeps stepping backwards and tries to land a couple of blows of his own, but he's missed most of them. Respectable, though. He may have no form, but he does know how to put his weight behind his punches. Tired of playing around, I grab him by the back of his head and slam my knee into his gut, forcing him to bend forward before I ram my body into him, knocking him on his back, giving me the upper hand.

But just as I am about to hit him again, I hear sirens, which forces me to look up, allowing him to kick me in the stomach, propelling me backwards.

As I realize the sirens are getting closer, I jump up to run, but a police cruiser has already pulled up. I know better, so I just stay still. I turn my head to look back toward Bex and her family but she and her mom are running toward her new boyfriend instead, offering him comfort. Her dad is just staring at me. I realize any ounce of respect he may have ever had for me is gone, but I also realize that I just don't care.

A police woman walks up to me and starts asking me questions, another officer walks over to Bex and her family and starts talking with them. More officers arrive, and the woman officer makes me sit on the curb while they begin to converse off to the side. One walks up and starts taking photos. Photos of him, of me, of the property. Another seems to be writing down statements from everyone. Before I know it, an older officer walks up to me and informs me that I'm under arrest and reads me my Miranda rights. He places me in cuffs and begins walking me to the patrol car.

"I'm gonna want a lawyer," I say, as he's putting me in the back seat.

I scan the scene one last time, and my eyes land on Bex's. She's watching me. She looks concerned. I find myself wondering if the concern means she still cares, but then she walks over to her new guy and puts her forehead against his. The anger begins to build inside me again. She doesn't care about me at all! I spend the rest of my time between her house and the jail thinking about how I'm going to make them pay. When I get out, they're going to regret this!

CHAPTER 17
Sherrye

There is a loud crack outside our house, followed by my daughter loudly gasping. I quickly look into the direction she's looking, but I don't see anything. However, Bex's reaction sends me into a spin. The way she screams Garrett's name sends a chill through me and sends me into protection mode. She's never really talked about what happened between them. Bex never opens up to me about anything anymore which I know is my own fault. But, I do know my daughter enough to understand that whatever happened, it was bad.

I see her running toward the door, and it makes me feel panicked, so I chase after her, and I feel my husband, Rick, close behind. He's hard on her, but I know he loves her just as much as I do.

"Leave now, Garrett!" I scream at him, "Get off our property or I'm calling the police!"

My hope is that will be enough to just scare him away, but to my shock, he grabs my daughter by the wrist and just yanks her toward him! What the hell? I feel my blood boiling and my pulse pounding. How dare he touch my baby girl? What the hell is this guy thinking?

"Let go of her!" I continue to yell at him.

I hear Garrett mumbling to her incoherently, begging her about something. My husband is starting to run toward them, but before he can get close to her, Zander comes rushing past and hits Garrett right in the face! Which seems to have taken him by surprise and he lets go of my daughter. I yell for my husband to call the police, as I run to Bex and just hold her.

The guys look like they are sizing one another up, and I'm hoping that the officers arrive before there is any more violence. I'm shocked by the turn of tonight's events. Things were going so well. The last thing I expected was to have Garrett show up and try to do, whatever it is he was trying to do to my daughter. I don't even know.

The thought of what she must have gone through with him makes my heart hurt for her. I feel like I've failed her. She clearly didn't feel comfortable enough to come to me about what was happening. I pull her closer to me and stroke her hair and she cries in my arms and continues to beg for Garrett to just leave. I feel myself starting to cry with her. She shouldn't be going through this. This is absolutely crazy to me.

The boys are continuing to exchange blows, but I'm worried because Garrett has Zander on the ground. I know Garrett is trained to fight, and he's significantly bigger than Zander. His protectiveness of my daughter has endeared him to me. I just hope the police hurry and arrive. My husband is still on the phone with them, and he hasn't been able to do much else to help Zander.

We hear the sirens coming closer, thank God! We see Garrett stumble backwards and fall to the ground. He begins to jump up with a very panicked expression. I think he's wanting to try to make a run for it, but it's too late for him. The officers arrive, allowing us to finally get to Zander to make sure he's okay. Thankfully, other than some swelling on his cheek and a small cut on his lip, he seems mostly fine.

The officers begin talking to everyone, including Garrett, to get our statements about what happened. They have someone come over and look at Zander's wounds, and then go check on Garrett's as well, before finally putting him in handcuffs and placing him in the car. Another officer is asking us if we want to press charges, I say yes, and then look over to Bex, who is still watching Garrett.

"Definitely," she says simply, followed with what almost sounds like a sigh of relief.

As the cop cars begin to pull away, I go inside to get an ice pack for Zander. When I come out, he and my daughter are hugging one another tightly. I feel relieved, not just because Garrett is finally gone but because she's happy. She's being held by someone who clearly loves her, cares about her, and would do whatever he can to try to protect her. I'd be lying if him being a doctor wasn't a great bonus! But still, even if he wasn't, this would be all I had to see to fully support this growing relationship my daughter has found herself in.

"Pardon me, guys," I say with a smile as I pull Zander back and place an ice pack on his face.

"Bex, are you doing okay?" I ask.

"I'm fine, mom. Just glad he's gone!" She gives me a small smile. "In fact," she goes on to say, "if you guys don't mind. I'd like to go take a hot bath and just process everything that just happened. Will you wait for me, Zander?"

He smiles at her and says, "Of course. Enjoy." She kisses his cheek and then leaves.

"Come inside, Zander. You can sit down and I'll get you some aspirin for the swelling and pain," I tell him.

He thanks me and follows me inside. After taking his seat, I bring him a drink, some aspirin, and a fresh ice pack. He thanks me again and smiles. I sit down beside him.

"Zander, I'm the one who should be thanking you," I begin.

He just looks at me, he's such a handsome young man. Between that and how sweet he is with her, I can see why Bex likes him so much. I've quickly grown to like him, as well. I think my husband has, too. He came in and gave Zander a pat on the shoulder before retiring to his room. That might not seem like much to people who don't know him well, but that was definitely him softening up.

"Zander, I know that when you first came in, I was being judgemental. You must understand that I am protective of my daughter. I worry for her," I say.

"Oh, it's okay. Don't worry about it, at all. I definitely understand," he says with a smile.

"Do you?" I ask. "Because, I was very wrong about you. I let preconceived notions get in the way of seeing who you really were. If someone did that to me, I wouldn't be as forgiving."

"No, I do. You want what's best for your daughter," he says with a look of understanding.

Part of me wants to continue to apologize, but I also want to know more about him, about Bex, too. I have so many questions, and I know I've missed out on so much with how closed off I've been. So instead, I change direction.

"How did you meet my daughter?" I ask.

"Well," he started, "your daughter's band opened up for mine. She's a great talent, and she blew me away with her command of the stage and her abilities. But, I didn't begin to get to know her until the next day, through her best friend, Tate and the rest of their band."

"Tate is certainly an interesting character!" I laugh.

"Ah, that she is, and she's a very good friend to Bex and me now, too. She was instrumental in helping protect Bex from her ex. You saw what he was like. It was rough," he said, with his smile fading.

"My daughter has clearly gone through stuff with him that we didn't know about. We had originally approved of him. He seemed to care about Bex. He had a promising career so we felt like he could take care of her, especially after her refusal to go to medical school. Which, I realize now that we should have never pushed her to do in the first place. It isn't what she wanted. Ultimately, we always just wanted her happiness. Clearly, Garrett has some serious problems." At this point, I'm not even sure I'm talking to him directly anymore, as much as just thinking out loud.

"Parents just want what's best for their kids. I understand that, I think Bex understands that, as well. You don't need to be too hard on yourself. Garrett had a lot of people fooled about who he was as a person. He certainly had Bex fooled. He was a manipulator, among other things. You can't fault yourselves for not seeing it," Zander offered, in an attempt to make me feel better.

In my mind, I'm thinking about what a kind young man Zander has turned out to be. He's generously offering me an olive branch, and I'm going to take it.

"So, tell me about your band," I ask, genuinely wanting to know about this boy who has stolen my daughter's heart.

He laughs, "Well, the short version is that music helps me blow off steam. One of the guys is my brother, so we used to just play around together. Over time, our friends would mess around with us and the sound just started coming together. One of the guys suggested we see about playing at this club, so we reached out to the owner, and we did it. We had a good reaction so we just kept doing it."

"But," he continued, "The longer story is that music helps me handle my job better. Sometimes the music helps me focus on coming up with the best treatment plans, sometimes it's great for celebrating victories for my patients, and sometimes, it helps me deal with the losses, too. And more recently, it's helped me figure out my feelings for your daughter. It's been my own personal therapy."

"And how did you get into medicine?" I ask.

"My grandmother had uterine cancer when I was younger. We didn't think she was going to make it, to be honest," Zander said, his eyes misting up, and his voice beginning to crack a little.

"But, she surprised us all," he continued with a laugh, "She is a feisty lady! A real fighter. She beat it. And, I knew what I wanted to do, right then and there. I had always known I wanted to do something to help women, but seeing my grandma beat cancer against the odds and ring that bell? I knew exactly what I wanted to do. I wanted to help women, and everyone really, ring the bell."

His compassion for others was heartwarming. I was so moved by his words, that my eyes began to tear up. He offers me a big, warm smile and gently pats my hand. Here I was trying to make him feel better, but he's trying to take care of me instead.

"I love my daughter," I say, with a smile.

Zander nods in support and understanding.

"Just so you know, I approve. And not, just because you're a doctor. But," I stop in an attempt to thoughtfully choose my words. "You're a good human, and I think you truly love my daughter."

"I think you're right," Zander says softly, with a big smile.

I hear Bex coming down the stairs, and I turn to face her. She's so beautiful. Even in her fuzzy pajamas with her wet hair. It makes me think of when she was just a little girl, when she would come bounding down the stairs after her bath. I find myself missing those days so much more often lately.

I walk over to my daughter and pull her close to me for a hug. She seems surprised at first, but I feel her just relax into my embrace, nuzzling up close.

"I love you, Momma," she sweetly says.

My eyes fill with tears. I'm overwhelmed thinking about how much I miss her and what she was going through. I wasn't there for her when she needed me, and it was my own damn fault.

"Oh Rebecca. I love you so much. I'm so sorry I wasn't there. I needed to be there for you when you were going through hell with Garrett. I should have been protecting you, but I didn't know. It's my fault."

Bex seemed taken aback by my comments, which hurt me more.

"Bex," I said, "I am so very proud of you. I don't tell you enough and I certainly haven't shown you enough."

She looked at me with a sweet smile, and said, "Momma, I'm proud of you, too."

We both laughed and hugged.

"By the way, Zander is a keeper," I whispered to her.

"I know," she laughed some more.

My heart feels full, relieved. I know my daughter is going to be okay. It's all I've ever truly wanted for her. I'm excited to see what the future holds for her. And, I'm even more excited that I will be there to watch it unfold. I make a vow to myself to be there for her

every step of the way, starting with her next concert.
I will not be missing that for the world.

CHAPTER 18
Bex

The past two weeks feel like they have flown by, and before you know it, we are back at the Skin and Bones for another show. Both Rock Chic and Facial Syndrome are premiering new music, thanks to the collaboration between the two bands.

I'm quite proud of how the songs have turned out. We have worked hard to grind out stuff that we can feel good about, and that we know our fans will feel good about, too. The overall mood of the two bands, and even Hawthorne, is one of excitement and perhaps a little bit of nervousness.

We've planned this show to a T, down to the very last detail. With us being off for a couple of weeks, we want to make a solid comeback. Rock Chic is up first, then we plan to close with one of our new songs. I'm looking forward to seeing the reactions from the crowd. It's nice to finally allow myself to fully enjoy being on stage without fear of repercussions.

Facial Syndrome will be joining us on stage to give our songs a richer sound. Much of the new stuff has a lot of layers to it, meant to create a more decadent experience, not just for the listener but for us, too. We love it! Afterward, we will leave the stage so that they can perform their set before we return for their new song, which we're pretty excited about. It's amazing, as well.

As we are climbing onto the stage for sound check, my friends notice my phoenix tattoo and several of the girls audibly gasp and the boys make a couple of strange noises. I purposefully wore a very short black skirt in hopes of this exact reaction. I act nonchalant about it, but inside I'm completely pleased.

As this is happening, Tate and Zander both quickly whirl around to see what has caught everyone's attention, and Tate lets out an exquisitely preposterous squeal and a wonderfully slow-moving, giant smile creeps across Zander's face.

Everyone crowds around to check it out as Zander leans in and whispers in my ear, "Wow. My beautiful phoenix is rising from the ashes. I'm so proud of you. It's perfect." Which makes the butterflies in my stomach go wild. I just smile at him. He's part of the reason I had the strength to make this leap. I don't even know if he realizes what a major role he has played.

Once I've finished distracting our bands, everything around begins moving like clockwork. The crowd seems to have picked up on the excitement in the air and we are vibing off of it.

They are really responding well to our set and especially the new song, which has us leaving the stage completely pumped. We are all smiles as we make our way through the crowd, we receive so many compliments and hugs, and people are just grabbing our hands.

Tonight has been amazing, and I can't wait to catch the guys' set now. Tate drags me to a table with a reserved sign on it that said Rock Chic. It was set up nicely, with beautiful flowers, small tealight candles in jars, and drinks arriving as soon as we approached. I look at her quizzically and she says Hawthorne saved the band a table up front to make it easier to get back on stage for the finale. That's fine with me.

It means I get to stare at this luscious man who has stolen my heart. That's right. My defenses are totally down. I watch him caress the microphone and stare at me like I'm the only woman in the room.

He's got these sexy little growls that melt me. *I think if he doesn't make a move soon, I may not be able to stop myself*, I giggle to myself. I'm not usually this bold. I must still be high off how incredible our show was!

Their show was amazing, the crowd is going crazy, and I think it's over. That last song was perfect. You can tell all the time and effort they put into it. I feel a lot of pride swell inside my heart for them. Harris, Ethan, and Tommy all leave the stage, but Zander stays behind.

He walks toward the side and, much to my surprise, gets out his acoustic guitar. I'm utterly confused because nothing that we've rehearsed included anything like this.

"So, this song is new, and it's for someone who has become quite special to me. I hope you all like it,"

Zander says in a voice just above a whisper before he looks my way and smiles sweetly. I hold my breath, anxious for what is about to come out of his mouth. Tate grabs my hand and squeezes. If I didn't know better, I would swear she knows what's happening. She's got a shit-eating grin on her face as the opening chords start.

> *"Tell me something that I know*
> *But want to understand.*
> *I need to hear it from your lips,*
> *I want to hear your plans.*
> *I want to offer you everything,*
> *From my heart to my hands.*
> *That I never could.*
> *Before today.*
>
> *We've made it through everything*
> *Thrown our way,*
> *Shared secrets and*
> *Put our hearts on display.*
> *But I love you,*
> *And I hope to hear you say...*
> *The words I never could.*
> *Before today.*
>
> *The morning sun drapes through your hair,*
> *As you stare into your coffee unaware,*
> *I can't speak, but the feeling is so rare.*
> *The words could not escape.*
> *Before today.*

This universe is just a big empty space
At night, when I am missing your face,
Everything I think to say
Disappears without a trace.
Couldn't put myself in a braver place,
Before today."

Is this...could this be about me? I'm speechless and even a little breathless. I can feel Tate looking at me, but I can't stop staring at Zander. The song is soft and beautiful and so different from either band's normal sound. I'm blown away. Suddenly, the song is over and the crowd is going wild. Zander smiles broadly and leans toward the microphone and says, "I love you, Bex."

I can no longer contain myself. I practically leap over the table to run up on stage and jump into his arms. "I love you, too! So, so much!" He kisses me and time stands still.

Or, at least until Tate walks on stage and whispers in his ear and reminds him we have one more song. He laughs and gathers us all on stage for our last song. I'm reeling, but I manage to hold it together and I swear we all played better than we ever have before.

After the show is over and we've loaded up our equipment, we have some time to mingle with the fans who, by and large, loved the acoustic song. Eventually, Hawthorne calls for the last call and we head toward the parking lot as he blasts,"Closing

Time" on the speakers. He's always known how to drop a hint.

I rode with Tate to Zander's house. This time I'm skipping the after-party again, but I know Zander and I have a lot to talk about. We will definitely make the next one. As we pull up, Zander and his brother are waiting for me. I give Tate a big hug and tell her that I will be talking to her in the morning. She laughs at me and gives me a wink. Ethan switches spots with me to ride with her to the after-party instead and they drive away.

I walk across the driveway toward Zander and slide my hand inside his, we have a lot to talk about. I don't know what the future holds for us, but I can't wait to find out.

EPILOGUE
Bex

Standing in front of the floor-length mirror, I can't believe what I am seeing. It doesn't seem possible that I am about to marry this beautiful, wonderful man. He came into my life when I was in danger. He took that danger away and helped me see that I deserve better. In learning to love myself, perhaps for the first time ever, I have fallen head over heels for Zander. He makes me feel like a princess. But not just any princess: an empowered superhero princess. Princess Leia, perhaps?

This morning was the perfect example of how wonderful Zander has been to me. I've been splitting time between my parents' home and his since Garrett went to jail. He was convicted of attempted kidnapping and stalking. He won't be around to bother us for a while, and I've got a protective order in effect for after he gets out. I more than just feel safe, I am safe. Finally, safe and free.

Last night, I was at my parents' home to spend one last night with them before I finish moving my things into my new home with Zander and his family. Other new brides might resent living with their new in-laws, but I adore how close Zander's family is. Even when they disagree, you can tell how deeply they love each other.

When I woke up and went downstairs for a cup of orange juice (okay, maybe a mimosa), much to my delight, I found a note addressed to me next to an arrangement of roses. I picked it up and smiled, before opening it.

Dear Bex,

Your wedding gift awaits you at the ceremony site. Don't be late!

With all the love I have in my heart to give,

Zander

I feel absolutely giddy! How could I possibly be late? I'm on my way to marry the man of my dreams *and* I get a present too! I'm an extremely lucky girl. I borrowed mom's car and I quickly drove myself to the site because I couldn't wait to get to my changing room to make sure everything was ready for me. Okay, obviously that wasn't the only reason I was in such a hurry. Tate promised everything would be in place and that she would be there soon to help me get ready. Of course, she never lets me down. So, I knew the preparations would be ready.

When I opened the door and walked in, there was a guitar case on the loveseat with a red ribbon that had my name airbrushed onto it. I squeal with delight as I open it and see the 1988 Alembic Stanley Clarke Signature bass I've been eyeing for so long. It was sold about six months ago and I thought it was gone forever, but it looks like my husband-to-be was the buyer. He is so amazing. I showed it to him once and he remembered it. My heart is filled with so much love and joy. My eyes fill up with tears, and I don't think I could possibly smile any wider.

I chuckle to myself, and my mother asks what is so funny as she straightens my veil. I can see the happy tears in her eyes and turn around to hug her close. Zander has not only healed me, he has also helped heal my family and it makes me love him even more. I never thought I'd ever feel as happy as I do now.

"Oh, just thinking back on the past year and looking forward to the future," I say.

Mom turns me around and pushes me back at arm's length and gets a serious look on her face. "Bex, I'm so sorry your father and I had been so hard on you. We have had high expectations your entire life and somewhere along the way, we forgot that you are your own person and you have to do what you know is best for you."

She continued," I will never push you to live up to what I want again, but I'm so glad you and Zander found one another. Your entire demeanor has changed since you have been together. Now you light up every room you enter. I have never seen you so confident and happy, and for helping you find that part of yourself, I will always love Zander."

I smile at my mom and just fall back into her arms. I'm proud of her, too. Words can never express what her and dad mean to me, so I don't say anything. I just hug her and cry. It's all I can really do for the moment.

With perfect timing, as always, Tate enters the changing room with her usual exorbitant flair, looking as stunning as always, and Mom quietly slips away to give me my last few moments with my bestie before the ceremony begins. She sits on the loveseat and pats the seat beside her. She also has tears in her eyes. I smooth my dress and sit quietly beside her, taking her hand.

"You look absolutely breathtaking, Bex, like an angel. A shockingly red angel but an angel none-the-less." She laughs, " I still can't believe that you are getting married. I'm so very happy for both you and Zander. You are so good for one another and I know you are going to have an amazing life together. And I can't wait to be Tia Tate!" she says with a wink and a grin.

"Whoa, whoa, whoa! Slow down, Tia Tate!" I protest. "Rock Chic is taking off. We are going to be touring and recording, and I am not doing any of that while pregnant or chasing toddlers. The band is still my baby.

I'm young and there's plenty of time to think of kids later. I'm still committed to my music, but now I'm dragging Zander along for the ride. Think he would make a good merch bitch?" The mental image of Zander pushing merch has us both cracking up with laughter.

"Maybe we can get him to wear the baby tee!" Tate laughs, while I wipe away the tears threatening to make my make up run.

A quick glance at the clock shows that the ceremony will be starting soon. I stand up and go back to the mirror to check my appearance one last time. I have grown my hair out just a little longer than my usual short style to a chin-length bob.

I've got soft beachy waves and a flower crown of red roses attached to a long flowing antique veil that once belonged to my grandmother. Of course, I dyed it to match my dress. But, the history makes it extra special to me.

My gown is embellished in a traditional style, but of course it had to have the Bex touch to make it my own. Nothing conservative for me! It's gorgeous and strapless with a tightly fitted silk bodice and long flowing skirt with a train. The skirt is covered in tulle flowers, and the flowers extend to the train, which is completely covered. I look almost like I'm being followed by a carpet of roses.

Oh, and the best part? The whole thing is red, veil and all. That's what makes it so absolutely perfect for me, and of course, mom and dad are happy with it too, which is a nice bonus. I smile, just as I hear a knock at the door. It's my father, telling me it's time. I take a deep breath and follow him out the door, and slide my arm into his. I'm pretty sure I saw a tear creep into my normally stoic father's eyes.

*****

Zander

As I'm standing near the minister, waiting for the ceremony to begin, I find myself getting nervous for the first time through this whole wedding process. I'm not nervous about our relationship, for that I have not a single doubt. I'm nervous about stammering over my vows or tripping over her dress as we go back up the aisle together. I'm nervous to have all eyes on us for what feels like one of the most sacred, personal moments of our lives.

Suddenly, the music is starting and I can't stop myself from holding my breath. First, my little cousins, Ramon and Isabelle, start their slow but clumsy walk down the aisle with the ring pillow and flower basket.

Ramon is obviously bored, but Izzy is having a ball throwing the flowers around willy nilly. I actually laugh out loud. Tate, as maid of honor, is escorted by my brother and best man, Ethan. They both look fantastic.

Then my breath catches in my throat, as Bex and her father appear at the end of the aisle. Bex is stunning. I mean objectively stunning and not just because I am so over the top in love with her. I'm not at all surprised that she has chosen all red from head to toe.

That's who she is, and it definitely works for her. I find myself studying every line, ruffle, and flower that embellishes my bride. She looks just like the phoenix I have envisioned her to be.

She's beautiful. I want to remember every moment, every shadow, every line of her as she is right now. We both have tears in our eyes as her father hands her off to me. We have chosen not to have the officiant ask who gives her away, as she's not property to be bought and sold. She is the strong, independent woman I fell in love with.

My mind is on autopilot during the entire ceremony because I'm finding that I can't really focus on anything but her. I'm getting lost in her eyes and the way that she is smiling at me the entire time. So, when it's time for the vows, I panic just a bit. This is the part that I'm afraid to screw up. When it's my turn to speak, I clear my throat nervously and let out a small laugh before I start.

"Bex, the first time I saw you, you were with your first love, your band. Your passion showed through in your bass lines and I was mesmerized. As I got to know you, I watched you grow into a confident beauty. We started as friends, but I knew that first night that I wanted to marry you someday.

I stood by your side in hope that you would one day feel the same. Now, I intend to be your husband for always. I will always protect you and be whatever you need in the hard times. I will not leave your side and I will cheer you on down whatever path you choose. I love you, Bex, and I'm so ready to start our lives together as husband and wife."

I take a deep breath in relief. I didn't screw it up! As I said them, the words were already imprinted on my heart. I knew them because every last one was true. Now, it's her turn.

"Zander, the first thing I remember about you is your gorgeous eyes in the crowd at our first gig together. I didn't get to actually meet you at that time but was not surprised when you showed back up in my life the next day. I wasn't ready to admit it yet, but now I believe it was destiny. You aren't perfect, but you are perfect for me. You mentioned my confidence, and it is true. I am much more confident now but that was your doing, Zander. Before you, I did not feel like I deserved someone so amazing. If asked, I would have said you were out of my league."

The guests laugh softly as she continues. "Zander, I pledge my heart to you for all time, even when you get a dad bod and start balding. I will support your dreams as you support mine, wholeheartedly. I will be your lover and your best friend. I can't wait for you to be my husband. Also, I'm very much ready to kiss you right now!"

I know the officiant must have declared us husband and wife, but I didn't hear him. Bex leaps into my arms and kisses me gleefully as the music starts and we run back up the aisle hand in hand as rose petals drop from the sky, and I didn't even trip.

The End

ABOUT THE AUTHOR

Jenna D Morrison is an up-and-coming author of fantasy, paranormal, and science fiction with a side of romance. She has been an avid reader since she was four and started writing for her own enjoyment in middle school.

She lives in Tulsa, Oklahoma with her mother and their very spoiled fur babies, American Pitbull. When she is not reading or writing, Jenna is a Zen Buddhist priest, an amateur genealogist, a daughter, sister, mother, grandmother, and aunt.

Kimberly A Campbell is a mother of four beautiful adult souls, grandmother to one amazing nine-year-old and has been a teacher to many young students that she loves as her own. She has always had a love for reading, writing and storytelling, advocating that same love in the children she's crossed paths with along the way. She's always dreamed of becoming an author, and is excited to finally have the opportunity to do so, with a focus on fantasy, paranormal and science fiction, which are her favorite genres. Kimberly makes her home in with her doting, supportive husband, children and many rescue cats in Houston, Texas. When she isn't reading, she enjoys spending time with her family, playing video games with her friends and baking delicious things she never eats.

Together, Jenna D. Morrison and Kimberly, best friends for nearly 20 years, write contemporary romance and young adult fantasy as Kenna Campbell.

Made in the USA
Middletown, DE
23 August 2022

72070553R10083